GONE-AWAY
LAKE

BY ELIZABETH ENRIGHT
Gone-Away Lake
Return to Gone-Away

Elizabeth Enright

GONE-
AWAY
LAKE

Illustrated by Beth and Joe Krush

———

HBJ

A Voyager/HBJ Book
Harcourt Brace Jovanovich, Publishers
San Diego   New York   London

Library of Congress Cataloging-in-Publication Data
Enright, Elizabeth, 1909-1968.
Gone-away Lake.
(A Voyager/HBJ book)
Summary: Portia and her cousin Julian discover summer
adventure in a hidden colony of forgotten summer houses
on the shores of a swampy lake.
I. Krush, Beth, ill. II. Krush, Joe, ill.
III. Title.
PZ7.E724Go 1987   [Fic]   86-29389
ISBN 0-15-636460-3

Printed in the United States of America

H I J K L M

To Oliver

CONTENTS

GONE-AWAY
LAKE

THE BEGINNING OF IT ALL

When Portia Blake and her brother Foster set out for Creston that summer, it was different from all the other summers. It was different because it was the first time they had ever made the trip all by themselves. Foster was only six-and-a-half, but Portia, as he said, was "beginning to be eleven."

"And that's old enough," she had persuaded her father and mother when they looked doubtful. "My goodness, what could *happen?* There are two of us, and Foster's all right to travel with. He just sits and looks out the window. He never howls and slams around the aisle like some boys do. He *behaves.* On a train, anyway."

Foster looked gratified and virtuous. "Let us," he begged. "Please? Mother? Daddy? Please?"

So here they were, side by side on a blue-plush coach seat, looking out of the window as happy and independent as two old people of thirty. Their mother and father had seen them off, of course, and spoken to the conductor about them, but all that seemed long ago. The city had already dwindled away, and country, real country, was skimming along beside the train. It was June, the very best ripest part of June; there were roses in all the yards and yellow flowers in all the fields. The trees were thick with leaves, and the grass still looked as soft as cloth because it was so new.

It was always June when they took the train to Creston, and they went every summer to stay with Uncle Jake Jarman and Aunt Hilda and their cousin Julian in the country. Their mother always went with them and their father came up later for a month; but this year, their parents were to be in Europe until August.

"Julian's an only child, poor thing," Portia had explained to her new school-friend Jody Harris. "But when we're there, he doesn't feel so only, I guess, and in winter he's at school, where he's captain of everything, so he makes out. He's twelve."

"What is he like?" Jody had asked.

"Well, he doesn't look at all like his name," Portia said. "I mean 'Julian' sounds like the name of a boy with dark hair, handsome and kind of aristocratic. To me it does, anyway—"

"I think it sounds like a man on a yacht," Jody said. "Some fat old man on a yacht."

"Well, *anyway*, Julian has straight red hair, not red but orange, really, and he wears a crew-cut that looks perfectly terrible. He has about a hundred thousand freckles on his face, all sizes, and the same color as his hair. *He* says it's the influence of the carrot on his appearance; he says that when he was a little kid, carrots were the only vegetable he'd eat, and he ate them every day for every meal except breakfast. So he turned orange. That's what *he* says, and then Uncle Jake always says: 'Good thing it was carrots and not spinach.'"

"That's not bad," said Jody, laughing.

"You'd never think to look at Julian that he's good at sports," Portia had continued. "The edges of his shirt sleeves are always too high up for his wrists, and the edges of his blue-jeans are too high up for his ankles, and he wears these terrible Keds that he kind of slaps around when he walks, like a penguin or something. But in spite of all that, he's captain of the school baseball team, and captain of the football team, and he can ski and figure-skate and do five kinds of fancy dive. He has these big front teeth that look as if he could bite a tree down, like a beaver, and he wears glasses. He's very, *very* nice."

"I guess he'd never be a success in the movies, though," Jody had said.

Now, in the train, Portia and Foster did not speak because they did not need to. They were both too happy. Portia was thinking about Julian and looking forward to seeing him again. The nice thing about him she often thought (and said) was that, though he was a member of the family and a boy, he wasn't half so fresh and bossy as an older brother would be. Some of her friends had terrible older brothers. Foster didn't count, of course. He was only six and a half and most of the time he was nice. But Julian was her favorite companion. He was, as Portia said, "crazy about Nature." He knew the names of all the birds, and of the different kinds of stones, and even of caterpillars and mosses. He was very nice, never condescending, about sharing this information with others. Portia wondered what he would be collecting this year. One year it had been snakes, one year cocoons and butterflies. Once he had kept three crawfish in a tank, and he *always* had turtles. . . .

"I can't *wait* to get there!" said Portia with an impatient bounce that jarred Foster but did not disturb him. He was thinking about Outer Space, which was what he often thought about. He had four different space helmets at home, and when he played by himself, you could hear him counting backwards: "Five, four, three, two, one. *Zero!* BLAST OFF!" And then he would gallop around the house holding up a toy space ship and making a noise like a vacuum cleaner, only he thought it was a noise like a space ship.

"Jupiter," said Foster quietly.

15

"What?" said Portia.

"Jupiter," repeated Foster. "That's the biggest one. I was just thinking."

"The biggest what?"

"Planet," said Foster.

"Honestly," sighed Portia. "Julian knows the names of all the things *in* the world, and you know the names of all the things *out* of it. What do I know, I wonder?"

Fortunately this depressing thought was interrupted by a waiter in a white coat who, like a one-man parade, pranced through the car beating a gong and calling news about lunch. Portia and Foster, who always got hungry the minute they set foot on a train, rose instantly and made their way to the dining car, where they were given a small table for two by the window. On the white cloth the knives and forks were gibbering quietly and ice was chiming in the glasses. Foster spread a great expanse of napkin over his front.

"I like this, don't you?" he said in a low voice. "It's so royal."

"I love it," said Portia, feeling very fond of her brother; and because of this, and because it was their first trip all by themselves, she let him have just what he wanted for his lunch, and that was pie. First he had a slice of apple pie and then a slice of blueberry, and for dessert he had another slice of apple but with a lump of vanilla ice-cream on top. Julian always said that Foster's two main interests were Outer Space and inner pie.

The waiter was a very nice man. "Son," he told Foster, "if you don't watch out, you're going to raise up in pie-hives." But of course they both knew he was joking.

As for Portia, she had what she always had on a train: a club sandwich that she could hardly get her mouth wide open enough to bite, and for dessert some of that train ice-cream that has to be whacked with a spoon before you can eat it.

Foster, surfeited with pie at last, leaned back in his chair and sighed comfortably. He was a nice-looking boy, Portia thought, faintly surprised. He had a calm face with very serious blue eyes. He had smooth brown hair, and when it was newly cut, as it was now, you could see two cowlicks, like two perfect little whirlpools on top of his head. His preferred attire was cowboy jeans decorated with jewels and nailheads, and bright checked shirts with insignias sewn to the sleeves. He wore sheriff's badges and space-cadet badges, and his belt was set with colored stones. Julian said that you should wear dark glasses when you looked at Foster in a strong light. But today, of course, because they were traveling, he was quieted down in a gray-flannel suit.

Portia didn't think much of her own looks. Too tan-colored. Tan skin with tan freckles. Tan straight hair with a bang in front. Even her eyes were a sort of tan, she thought. The brightest thing about her face was the new tooth-braces that showed when she smiled. She was a thin girl and not very tall, but never mind, she assured herself fiercely; I'm going to grow up *gorgeous*, no matter what. I'll just wish myself into it.

After lunch they went back to their own car, which was named the *Benjamin X. Hawley*.

"Whoever *he* was," Portia said.

"Maybe he was the inventor of the train," Foster suggested.

"Maybe he was the inventor of the club sandwich," Portia said, and for some reason this seemed very witty to both of them. They went snorting and giggling along the aisle to their seat, as the blank grown-up faces stared at them.

"How far is Creston now?" Foster asked. He had been asking this question steadily every five or ten minutes since they had left the city.

"About an hour away," said Portia.

They sat in silence. Cows, towns, and fields flew by. After a while Foster began to get sleepy. His sister could tell by his eyelids, which always got thick-looking, and by the yawns that he kept trapped in his mouth. It was infectious; soon she was trying not to yawn herself.

But when, finally, the train had left the last station before Creston, and they had carried their suitcases to the door, they were both wide-awake. A smell of country came into the train, and it was a smell that they never got used to; Foster began hopping and twitching with excitement, and Portia had to hold onto him.

"Crest*on!* Crest-on!" bawled the conductor, a grave fatherly-looking man whose ability to bellow came as a surprise.

"Look, there they are, there they *are!*" cried Portia, al-

most bellowing herself. "It's them! It's Julian and Uncle Jake!"

They glimpsed two upturned faces and lost them. The train went on for a little, slowly, and with a great double-jointed clatter and bang managed to stop. Portia and Foster scrambled down the iron steps, dragging their bags.

"Hi!" shouted Uncle Jake, sweeping Foster up into the air, bag and all.

"What have you got in your mouth?" was the first thing Julian said to Portia.

"Tooth braces," she told him, stretching the sides of her mouth to give him a better view.

"Holy cat! When you smile, it looks just like the front of a Buick!" Julian said.

Now probably if a brother had said that, she would have been mad, Portia thought. But he didn't say it the way a brother would have; he said it politely, and she agreed with him. When she smiled, it did look just like the front of a Buick.

"Hey, guess what!" was his next remark. "Katy's got puppies!"

"No!" cried Portia. "How glorious! How many?"

"Five, all sooty-faced."

"Can I have one?" asked Foster.

"You and Portia can pick one out to own together if your parents agree to it," said Uncle Jake, who was a wonderful

man, and Foster gave a lurch into the air, signifying joy.

Katy was the Jarman's boxer dog. Portia considered her the most human-looking animal she had ever seen. Her face looked like a very dark sad *person's* face attached to the body of a dog. When she was younger, Portia had been fond of pretending that Katy really was a person who had been enchanted into a dog: a princess, or a little girl from Africa, or someone. She had almost believed it, too, because in those days she had almost believed in magic.

"How glorious!" she said again.

"There are four males and one female," Uncle Jake said. "They're just beginning to stagger around and chirp. We waited for you to help name them, Portia."

Uncle Jake was an enormous man with a mustache. He liked children, and children always liked him. He had taken Portia's bags from her and was now stowing them away in the back of the good old car that Portia had known almost as long as she could remember.

"This car always smells exciting," said Foster when they were inside it, and Portia knew just what he meant.

They drove through Creston and then on through the village of Attica and beyond, for this year the Jarman family had a new house, a bought one. Before this they had always had a rented one in Attica, where Uncle Jake published the local paper, *The Attica Eagle;* but the new house, Aunt Hilda had written, was deep in real country.

"It's not really new, though," Julian explained. "I mean it was built about fifty or sixty years ago. It's neat. There are woods in back, and there's a brook that you can practically swim in. Dunk in, anyway."

The June countryside looked very beautiful to the Blake children: soft grass rippling and running in the meadows; different kinds of roses on all the fences; and then at last no meadows *or* fences, only woods, until they came to a driveway and turned in. The name Jarman was painted on the mailbox.

There were trees on each side of the drive. A bird flashed among them, red as a stop light.

"Scarlet tanager," said Julian in a proprietary way, as if he, personally, were responsible for its appearance.

"Are we almost there?" asked Foster. He was beginning to look rather bleached around the mouth, and Portia knew that all the pie and excitement and driving were making him feel sick at his stomach.

"Just around the next bend," said Uncle Jake.

"You'll be all right," Portia told Foster. She certainly hoped he would be. And then, luckily, they did round the bend and the woods opened out, and there was the Jarmans' old new house. It looked just right: big enough, but not too big; and it had all different sorts of windows; dormers and bays and the ordinary kind. Vines grew thick on the clapboards, and there were many trees and a large lawn patched with flowers. There was a croquet set on the lawn. There was a swing hanging down from a tree.

"We fixed that up for Foster," said Julian, as if he were too grand and elderly for that sort of thing himself.

Katy was on the front steps waiting. As they drew up, she barked "hello" the way she always did. She had a deep hollow-sounding dignified bark as if she were addressing them from the basement of a castle. Portia and Foster flung open the car doors and fell out, and Katy jumped up on them, kissing their faces and snuffing dew all over them and talking a little in dog-talk, the way she knew how to do when she was happy. She was a very welcoming dog.

Next came Aunt Hilda in a lavender dress.

"Oh, darlings, how wonderful to have you back!" she cried, running down the steps and hugging them. She was a very welcoming aunt.

"Ma, take a look at the hardware display in Portia's mouth," said Julian. "Show her, Porsh."

"Well," said Aunt Hilda. "It looks very costly, very valuable. And it will give you a beautiful smile later on."

Aunt Hilda was Portia's third favorite woman in the world. First came her mother, naturally, and after that came Miss Hempel, her English teacher, and after that came Aunt Hilda; but she was so close behind Miss Hempel that it was more of a tie, really.

"Now, before we even show you the house, we must introduce you to Katy's children," Aunt Hilda said, and she led them around the house to a cellar door and down the steps to a big, clean basement. And there in an old baby-pen were the puppies.

They had little dark flat faces like pansies, and ears that felt like pieces of silk, and claws like the tips of knitting needles. Portia had to pick one up first thing. It had a round little stomach and wrinkled paws, and it nipped her finger gently and growled an imitation growl.

"Any ideas for names yet? Any inspirations?" said Uncle Jake.

"I'll have to watch them for a while till I learn their characters," Portia said rather importantly. She knew she was supposed to be quite good at naming things.

Katy, who had followed them down, jumped over her own low place in the railing and counted the puppies with her nose to see that no one was missing. Then she lay down on her side, and they lined up along her to nurse.

When Portia went upstairs and in the front door, the first thing she saw was the Jarmans' cat Thistle. (She had named him, for instance.) He was sitting on the newel post looking huffy.

"He's put out about the puppies," Uncle Jake said. "No one makes a fuss over him any more."

"Well, I'll make a fuss over you," Portia said loyally, and picked the big lazy cat from the newel post. He was just as soft and limp as somebody's old fur-piece, and all his paws hung down like empty socks. He opened his mouth and yawned in her face, but she hugged him and tickled him under the chin, and soon, in spite of himself, he began to purr.

"Well, but come and see the *house*, for Pete's sake!" said Julian, and Portia let Thistle drop down gently. He shook first one ear, then the other, and walked away disgustedly, as if the floor was damp under his paws.

All the rooms in that house were big and light and comfortable. Each piece of furniture in the living room was as familiar to Portia as a member of the family: the good old couches and the good old chairs, all wearing new slip-covers; and the piano in which, under the strings, there was a petrified cough-drop, and she was the only one who knew about it. (It had fallen out of her mouth once when she was four years old, playing on top of the piano. She had been playing raft.)

There was a sun porch and a plain porch, and a huge kitchen that smelled of cinnamon and had two stoves: a coal one and a gas one.

Upstairs, when they showed her the room she was to have, Portia gave a scream of pleasure. "All my *life!*" she cried dramatically. "Aunt Hilda, all my *life* I've wanted a bed like that!"

"It's got a roof on it like a Conestoga wagon," said Foster. "Yikes, what do you want a roof on a *bed* for?"

"Because it's beautiful; it's like a tent," explained Portia reasonably.

"Look what's right outside your window, though," said Julian, and when she did, she saw a nest on a branch close to the sill, and on the nest a bird was sitting: gray, with a shimmer of pink on its neck. She could have touched it.

"Mourning dove," Julian said. "That's the male sitting. They make the worst nests in the world, those birds. The way a *kid* would make a nest, I mean. Amateurish."

He was right. The nest was hardly more than a platform of little sticks stuck together any old way. (All that month, whenever there was a storm or a sudden wind, Portia worried about that nest and its occupants the way she remembered her mother worrying about Foster when he had croup. She kept running up to her room to see if all was well. "You act like you're their aunt, or something," Julian told her. But in the end the baby birds grew up safely and flew away.)

After they had examined all the bedrooms—Foster's had one with a double-decker bed, which was the kind *he'd* always wanted—and the attic, Julian took them out of doors and showed them about. There was a big hollow tree, and a brook with stepping stones, or rather leaping stones, and a bent-over birch tree that you could swing on, and an oriole's nest that had real orioles in it, and a praying mantis's nest that had real praying mantises in it, so Julian said, but they didn't show.

After a while they went down to the basement and played with the puppies till suppertime, and after supper they played croquet till the stars came out and the bats began to zip through the dusk as if they were cutting out fancy patterns.

When Portia was in bed, she could smell that smell of nighttime in the country. She heard an owl making a spook-noise far away, and a whippoorwill croaking and croaking in a tree nearby. She felt peaceful and comfortable in her tent bed.

Of course she did not dream that the next day was going to be so exciting.

2

THE STONE AND THE SWAMP

The next morning when she woke up, Portia saw sunshine at the window. A big fly was buzzing and whining up and down the screen, and she could smell bacon and coffee. She felt glad to be where she was, with the summer just beginning, and for a few minutes she simply lay there listening to the fly and feeling happy.

Then she got up suddenly, with a bound, and began putting on her comfortable summer clothes: her old country jeans and a T-shirt and some sneakers. "No more socks, thank goodness," sang Portia. "No more DRESSES!" She unhooked the screen and opened it. The big fly zizzed off into the sunshine. The mother mourning-dove was on the nest looking as neat and soft as a pair of folded gloves.

When she went downstairs, Thistle was sitting outside the screen door waiting. (In the country something or somebody always wants to come in or get out.) Portia let him in and plucked a cobweb from his whiskers. He'd been out all night and smelled of the woods.

At the Jarmans' house they always had breakfast in the kitchen, and Aunt Hilda was a talented creator of breakfasts. She remembered about things like waffles and blueberry muffins and sausage cakes. Today there were waffles, and for a long time there was no conversation but: "Please pass the butter," or "More syrup, please."

Just as they were finishing, groaning a little, there was a

knock at the door. They looked up to see a boy about Foster's age. His apparel was strikingly like Foster's, too. He had a cowboy hat on the back of his head, and four pistols stuck into his belt, and a plastic ray-gun in his hand. "I heard there's a guy here who likes to play Space," he announced.

Foster rose from his chair. "I'm who he is," he told the boy.

"Good morning, Davey," said Aunt Hilda. "This is David Gayson who lives on the next farm. These are Julian's cousins, Davey: Foster and Portia Blake. Would you like a waffle?"

"No, I ate," said Davey. Boys take longer than girls to learn about thank-you, thought Portia.

By this time Foster was outside the door.

"I know where there's a neat hollow tree we could use for a stage-rocket," he told Davey.

"Yikes! Blast off, men," yelled Davey, and away they went.

"I'd better be blasting off myself," said Uncle Jake, who had been very silent. He always came to the surface slowly in the morning. He gave Aunt Hilda a kiss good-by and waved to Portia.

When she was drying the dishes, Julian came down from tidying up his room. Portia knew what that meant. It simply meant that he made his bed and threw everything that was on the floor into the closet. (Except when Aunt Hilda caught him, of course.) And anyway his room never could look neat because of "the collections." The bureau was crowded with caterpillar jars, and the shelves with birds' nests and cocoons on twigs, and on the mantelpiece there was a procession of minerals. Mounted specimens of butterflies and moths hung in cases on the walls, and over the bed five tacked-up snakeskins were tastefully arranged. The turtles occupied a tank cozily situated beside the wastebasket.

"You want to come collecting with me, Porsh?" said Julian.

26

"Portia's a terrible name," she said. "There's no nickname for it but Porsh. That's what I have to listen to people calling me. Porsh. Okay, sure. Of course I want to. But what are you collecting?"

"Oh, what I find," he said airily. "I'll take my bird guide and the field glasses and the butterfly net and the killing jar. You can carry the killing jar."

"Thanks," said Portia.

Aunt Hilda made them a picnic lunch. She packed it into Julian's creel, and he had that hanging down in back of him and his field glasses and camera hanging down in front, so that he clashed and jingled when he walked. "Like a horse in some kind of a harness," Portia said.

"Where are we going?" she asked as they came out of the house.

"I don't know. We'll start off through those woods beyond the garden; I've never been all the way through them yet."

They walked up the slope into the woods and kept on walking up. It was a wonderful day. The leaves rustled softly and endlessly in the wind. Everything was moving in those woods: all the leaves and all the twigs and all the birds. And the sunshine was sliding and jumping in patches over the ground. Julian showed Portia where there was a bee tree, and they saw another tanager and an indigo bunting and a fox. The fox was the best thing.

Just as she did on a train, Portia always became hungry on a picnic much sooner than she would have at home. This also was true of Julian, fortunately. They came unexpectedly upon a round clearing among the trees, and in the center there was a great boulder coated with moss and tufted with ferns.

"Let's have our lunch up on that!" said Portia. "How do you suppose it ever got there, anyway? Maybe it's a meteorite!"

"No such luck," said Julian. "Nothing's ever a meteorite;

everything's always a rock. I've been looking for a meteorite ever since I was a child of five. I wonder where they all drop to?"

"Oh, into the ocean and Texas and Siberia and places like that probably," said Portia.

They climbed up on the boulder. It was hot and sunny up there, and they disturbed a large community of ants; not the biting kind luckily, though they did turn out to be the kind that get into sandwiches, as they soon discovered.

"They don't bother me any," Julian said with his mouth full. "I bet I've eaten a hundred thousand ants in my time."

"It's them I'm thinking about," Portia told him. "What a horrible death!" And she picked as many out of her sandwich as she could and helped them escape.

The deep woods shimmered and stirred in a wall around them; the sunny rock smelled of baked moss. There was icy ginger ale in the thermos bottle ("instead of just usual old milk," Portia said), and for dessert there were homemade cupcakes with orange frosting.

"Hey! There're garnets in this rock," said Julian suddenly. Portia scrambled over to see. It was true. The rocky seams of stone were studded with little hard lumps the color of grape jelly. Julian took out his Scout knife and gave Portia the nail file attached to his pocket knife (a fixture he seldom used), and they began trying to chip some out of the rock.

"We'll take them home to Ma," Julian said. "She can make 'em into a thing for around her neck or something."

It took quite a while to chip a few of them loose, and the sun was pouring down on their backs as they worked. It was noon.

"Ho-ly cat!" shouted Julian all at once. "Porsh! Look! Ho-ly cat!"

"What now?" said Portia. "You're the most emotionable boy I ever knew."

He was pointing with his knife. "Look! Someone's carved letters into the rock! I scraped away the moss, and there they were!"

On the face of the rock, deeply cut, Portia read these words:

LAPIS PHILOSOPHORUM

TARQUIN ET PINDAR

15 JULY 1891

"Eighteen-ninety-one!" said Portia. "All that long time ago! But what does it mean, I wonder?"

"I don't get Latin till first year High," Julian said. "But that's Latin, all right, and I know from my geology books that *lapis* means stone. And *philosophorum* must mean something about a philosopher. I know; philosopher's stone! That's what it must mean, philosopher's stone! . . . But I don't understand the *Tarquin et Pindar* deal at all."

"What is a philosopher's stone, anyway?" asked Portia. "And what's a philosopher in the first place?"

"Someone who knows a lot. A guy that studies a lot, and has wisdom and stuff like that. Kind of a wise, calm guy. And the philosopher's *stone* was supposed to be a magic stone or rock that would turn any metal, tin or lead even, into gold. Of course there never was any such thing."

"How do you know? How do you know that this isn't it?" Portia was terribly excited. "Let's try it on something now!"

"Listen, brain," said Julian in a scornful exasperated way, almost like a brother. "If it had been a real philosopher's stone, these knives we've been using would both be turned to gold right now. See? And all they still are is steel."

Of course he was right. Portia felt embarrassed.

"But it certainly is an interesting thing to find," he said. "I wish I knew who'd carved the words, though. Gosh, I'd give anything to know!"

"And *why* they did it," Portia agreed. "Do you think that maybe *et* means *and* the way it does in French? Tarquin *and* Pindar? Could those be names?"

"They could, I guess, but pretty goofy ones. Now if it said Bill *et* George, you'd *know*."

They puzzled over the mystery in the hot, still sunshine. Finally, feeling too warm, they climbed down and started on their way again. For a long time they kept to the backbone of the wild tangled ridge but at last started zigzagging down the farther side. They found a dead tree with funguses sticking out of it in balconies and terraces. Julian cut off the largest one to keep; and a little later he caught a Catocala moth, whose dowdy upper wings concealed a beautiful scarlet pair beneath, like two geranium petals. When he popped it into the killing jar, Portia had to look away. She hated to see it killed, but it was dead in less than a second, and then she didn't mind any more.

At the foot of the hill the woods kept on going. Portia and Julian kept on going, too.

"Man, am I lost!" Julian said. "So are you. I don't know where we are at all!" He sounded very happy about this. Portia didn't mind herself; it was daytime and summertime and she was with him.

When they discovered a brook curling through the woods, they decided that they needed to go wading. The water still had its winter coldness. "It's just one degree up from ice!" Julian said. Their feet looked green in the water, but when they lifted them out, they were lobster-red. On the floor of the brook there were many caddis cases made of twigs and mica-flakes. Julian collected a few, putting them into the thermos bottle with some brook water.

"We've done pretty well today," he said. "We've got the Catocala and these caddis worms and the tree fungus and the garnets. But the sensational thing is the philosopher's stone!"

"And the fox that we saw," said Portia.

After a while they put on their sneakers and started off again, stepping lightly. "My feet feel as if there were spangles all over them," Portia said.

For a long time they followed the twisting brook. "Am I ever lost!" Julian repeated happily; but Portia said: "Look! We're coming out; there's sunshine ahead."

It was true. The woods were ceasing, slowly, tree by tree; and in a few minutes they found themselves out in the open, a tall forest of grass confronting them. No, it was not really grass, but a vast swaying growth of reeds and rushes, all taller than they were. And as they pressed forward, their footsteps began to have a gulpy sound, and the brook fanned itself out and was lost in the thick moss that grew between the stems.

"A swamp!" cried Julian. "Nobody ever told me that there was this great big swamp—wait! Look at that—!"

31

"At what?" said Portia.

But Julian was suddenly jingling and squelching and banging away through the reeds and rushes, and as he lunged and stumbled, he was unfolding his net. "Butterfly!" he shouted over his shoulder.

"You mean that dopey little brown thing?" said Portia, galloping at his heels. "Why, it's not even pretty!"

"Rare though, brother. Shut up now, please—there! Nope, got away; but I'll *get* it!"

He kept hopping and plunging this way and that, and Portia hopped and plunged close behind him. To be lost with somebody is one thing; to be lost by yourself is something else.

Julian stopped short and hissed at her to stop, too. He began crouching forward inch by inch, then pounced with the net.

"Oh, man! I got him! I *got* him!"

Into the jar went the poor brown butterfly. Portia turned away again, and then it was dead and she could look at it: small, brown, inconspicuous.

"Rare, though," Julian repeated. "All you women think about is the looks of things: what's *pretty*, and stuff like that. Nonessentials."

On a common impulse they had seated themselves on a large coarse hassock of grass. Their feet were ankle-deep in water, but it didn't matter; their shoes had already been soaked, and this was swamp water, warm from the sun.

Julian kept turning the jar and gloating over his new prize.

"My heavens, you'd think it was made of uranium, or something," Portia said.

A plume of gnats moved unevenly in the air above their heads. From it came a thousand tiny needle-points of sound, all of them together making one small music. Now and then a finger of wind stirred in the reeds. It was good to rest there with the sun on their heads and their feet in the soup-warm water. It was peaceful.

But not for long. Every mosquito in the swamp seemed to have been alerted at the same moment, and now they appeared from all directions: out of the reeds, up from the water, down from the sky, whining voraciously.

"They're the size of helicopters!" yelled Julian, leaping to his feet. "We've got to get out of here!"

They began running through the slapping reeds, though they had no idea where they were going; they couldn't see.

Julian was ahead as usual, and all at once he crashed into some hidden obstacle and fell over it. Even as he was falling, he held the killing jar up so that it wouldn't get broken. Then he looked at his camera to see if it was damaged, and then at his field glasses to see if they were, and when he found that nothing was, he took the time to say "Ow!" and rub his shinbone.

"What hit me?" he said.

"You hit it," Portia said. "And for heaven's sake, look, it's a rowboat! An old upside-down rowboat buried in weeds!"

"What the heck is it doing here? You can't go rowing on a swamp! But maybe if I stand up on the thing, I can see where we are, at least."

They both climbed up on the little hulk and looked out over the tops of the reeds, a sea of reeds, beyond which, and all around, grew the dark woods. But that was not all. Portia and Julian drew in a breath of surprise at exactly the same instant, because at the northeast end of the swamp, between the reeds and the woods, and quite near to them, they saw a row of wrecked old houses. There were perhaps a dozen of them; all large and shabby, though once they must have been quite elaborate, adorned as they were with balconies, turrets, widows' walks, and lacey wooden trimming. But now the balconies were sagging and the turrets tipsy;

the shutters were crooked or gone, and large sections of wooden trimming had broken off. There was a tree sticking out of one of the windows, not into it but *out* of it. And everything was as still as death.

"Now who would go and build a lot of houses on the edge of a mosquitoey old swamp like that?" inquired Julian. But the next time he spoke it was in a whisper. "Porsh! Those houses are empty! They're all deserted, Porsh! It's a ghost town."

"Oh, let's go, let's go!" Portia whispered back, pulling at his sleeve. "I don't like it here!"

But Julian frowned and jerked his sleeve away. "Just a minute, now. Ju-u-ust a minute. We'd better examine the situation. Case the joint, in other words."

"Oh, please come, please!" begged Portia. Her voice quavered with fear, almost with tears, but she was beyond pride.

"Sh-h. In a second," whispered Julian.

And just at that moment, in the last house on the right-hand side they heard a curious crackling sound; and then an enormous voice began to speak.

3

GONE-AWAY

They were so startled that they fell through the boat. The wood was damp and rotten, and then perhaps the panic of surprise had added a sudden weight to them. In any case they fell through with a crash; and it was as they were hastily picking themselves out and wondering if they were hurt anywhere that they heard the words the mighty voice was addressing to the summer air. They stared at each other in amazement.

"Yes, friends—" roared the great suave tones. "Why suffer any longer from acid indigestion? *Go* to your local drugstore, now, today, and ask for a box of Pepso-Tabs, the wonder mint, only forty-nine cents the box. Yes, friends, in exchange for only *for-ty-nine cents*—your troubles are over!"

Julian was the first one to laugh.

"Whoever heard of a ghost having acid indigestion?" he said.

Portia was laughing, too. "And whoever heard of ghosts listening to radios?" she said. "It must be a radio, Jule, because I didn't see any television-tree on the roof, did you?"

"Wait a minute." Julian climbed precariously up on an edge of the boat, as Portia held onto him.

"No," he reported. "And now that I look at it, I can see that *that* house isn't quite as raggedy and bashed-in looking as the others. They've got a screen door, and there's a rosebush and some bean-rows, and now I see some chickens and a duck. . . . Come on, Porsh, let's go see who lives there and ask them where we are—"

"Oh, I don't know—do you think we'd better?"

"Sure! It'll be all right. Would bad people keep a duck? Would they have a *rose*bush?"

Portia was not entirely happy about the logic of this assurance, but she had no choice except to follow her cousin who had started forward with a determined step.

In the house someone had turned down the huge radio voice; all they could hear now was a low steady babble and some little chicken-noises.

The children pressed their way among the cool leathery reeds; a few obstinate mosquitoes accompanied them, and every now and then there was the sound of a slap or an exclamation.

Julian, who paid certain penalties for persistently taking the lead, now banged his knee smartly against the corner post of a little overgrown landing dock.

"You know what *I* think," he said, when the pain stopped ringing. "*I* think this swamp must have been a pond or a lake once upon a time. That would account for the rowboat and this dock and all—"

"And for those houses being built where they are."

"Check. But I never *heard* of any lake around here."

"You haven't lived here very long, remember."

They climbed up on the dock and walked it gingerly, on the lookout for loose or missing planks. The reeds that waved above their heads had been replaced by a growth of plumed pampas grass, still taller, but now as they broke through the last of this, they found themselves on raised land, close to one of the wrecked houses. It was not the one they had been aiming for; apparently they had veered a little from their course. Now that they were close to it, they could see what a ruin the old house was, with broken windows and loose-toothed shutters. Someone, tramps perhaps, had carved initials into the porch railing, and on one of the square porch pillars a crop of fungus stuck out like turkey feathers—just such fungus as they had found on the dead tree in the woods.

"It looks haunt-y," said Portia, drawing close to her cousin. "I'd hate to be here at night. It's bad enough in plain real day."

In the tangle of rough grass and daisies and butter-and-eggs they saw that there was a narrow footpath leading to the house at the right, and they threaded their way along this (Julian, of course, in the lead). As they approached, they could hear the radio more clearly: "Marcia, I can't go on, I tell you! I don't know what to *do* without him; I don't know what to DO!" . . .

The hens gave a squawk when they saw the children and skedaddled out of the way. The duck took matters more calmly, warping herself sideways, like a little ferryboat, to the shelter of a large dock-leaf. There she folded her flat feet under her and settled down comfortably, looking more like a boat than ever. The rosebush was in full bloom; its flowers were yellow; and beyond it there was a great burst of scarlet Oriental poppies.

Portia and Julian hesitated, then walked up the two quavery porch steps, hesitated again, and knocked at the patched screen-door. The breath of the house came out to them. It smelled old.

"Pindar?" called a voice inside. "Is that you?"

"Pindar!" whispered Julian. "The name on the rock!" Aloud he replied: "No, ma'am, it's not. It's us."

"Well, who in the world—" said the voice. The radio was abruptly silenced. They heard small steps in the house, and out of the dimness a figure approached: a small, thin old lady. The first thing they noticed about her was the queerness of her clothes: they seemed like fancy-dress clothes, so old-fashioned and long and sweeping. She was wearing a dress of black-and-white striped silk; it had leg-of-mutton sleeves and a high-boned collar made of lace. Her white hair, curled in multitudes of little pleaty ridges, was dressed in a pompadour, and on top, like a small vessel on a choppy sea, a red velvet bow was riding.

The old lady had eyeglasses fastened to a chain; as she approached, she fumbled for these and placed them astride her nose—a formality of some sort, surely, since she looked at Portia and Julian not through the lenses but over them.

"Children!" she cried. "Why, it's two real *children!*" She sounded as surprised as if she had found herself confronted by a pair of armadillos, though perhaps more pleased, for now she smiled; a whole lacey set of smiling wrinkles came into view as she opened the door. "Come in, children, come in. Why, what a treat, I do declare. What a *treat!*" Her eyes were black and sparkling. They liked the way she looked.

"I hope we didn't startle you too much, ma'am," said Julian, who often had very courtly manners away from home.

"No, goodness, oh, dear me, no! Why it's wonderful to see real children again; it's been years since—but come in, please, do come into the sitting room, won't you? It so seldom gets sat in!"

"Well, we really should be on our way—" murmured Julian, following her, however, with Portia following *him*.

The old lady opened a door at the left of the hall and ushered them in.

Their first impression was one of density. A large herd of furniture grazed on a red carpet; each wall was covered with a different kind of wallpaper, one patterned with roses, one with ferns, one with stripes, and the fourth, Julian thought, with things that looked like bunches of broccoli. On the wallpaper many large pictures stared out of heavy frames. The windows in the room were half-hidden by plants and vines in hanging baskets and curtained with old dark velvet portieres. Everything that could have a cover on it had one. An upright piano in one corner stared out

38

from under a draped arrangement of fringed plush like a severe Turkish lady. All the tables had covers on them, of course, and the chairs and couches each had a collar and a set of cuffs.

"All this came out of the Big House," said their hostess, as if this explained everything. "Now sit down, do, and tell me wherever in the world you *came* from? How did you get here?"

"Through that swamp out there," said Julian. "We were a little bit lost."

"We were entirely and absolutely lost," said Portia.

"But not through the *swamp!*" cried the old lady, clapping one leaflike hand to her cheek.

"Why, yes, we—"

"Oh, but that's *dangerous*. There's a spot somewhere in it (my brother swears it shifts its position almost daily) that a man could drown in; cattle *have* been sucked in and drowned. Tell me, where do you come from?"

"Back that way," said Julian, gesturing vaguely. "Back through the woods and over that long hill. We live about halfway between Attica and Pork Ferry."

"Well, my brother can show you a safer way to go home when the time comes. May I ask your names?"

"I'm Julian Jarman and *she's* Portia Blake."

"We're cousins," said Portia.

"Now isn't that nice!" said the old lady. "If cousins are the right kind, they're best of all: kinder than sisters and brothers, and closer than friends."

Portia was surprised. She had supposed that this was her own personal discovery.

"My name is Cheever," said their hostess. "Minnehaha Cheever. Mrs. Lionel Alexis Cheever."

"How do you do," said Julian.

"How do you do," echoed Portia, glittering her tooth braces politely.

"I wonder if you could tell us, ma'am—uh, Mrs. Cheever

—just exactly where we are," inquired Julian. "I mean we're still lost."

"Well, this place used to be called Tarrigo Lake, when it *was* a lake. That was a long time ago, though. Nowadays folks call it Gone-Away. Gone-Away Lake."

"See, what did I say, Porsh? It was a lake once!" exclaimed Julian proudly, as if she had argued the matter.

"Oh, a beautiful lake," said Mrs. Cheever. "Small but clear, and blue as—blue as—laundry bluing! Boats on it! Boats like butterflies skimming and dipping. We had one; Papa did. The *Trixie II.* I was too young to know the *Trixie I.* And tennis courts; and the Club; twelve families in all. Or was it thirteen? No, twelve. Every summer we all came and stayed from June the first to September the fifteenth. . . ." She fell silent for a moment. "Well, it's hard to believe how alive it all was. Oh, the parties we had! The picnics on Craneycrow—"

"Craneycrow?" said Julian.

"That was an island—well, it still is—right in the middle of Tarrigo. We called it that, because of the old rhyme, remember?

> "*Chickama, Chickama, Craneycrow*
> *I went to the well for to wash my toe.*
> *When I got back my chicken was gone.*
> *What time is it, old witch?*"

"I never heard that before," Portia said.

"You didn't? It's part of a game. Maybe children don't play it any more, or maybe they only play it in the South. It was Baby-Belle Tuckertown who taught it to us, and *she* came from Tennessee. . . . So on the island there was a little old house that nobody lived in; we thought it had a witchful look, and that's why we named the place Craneycrow."

"Is the house still there?" asked Portia.

"I shouldn't wonder, but I don't know for sure. That

island's so smothered in evergreens that you can't see anything else, even in winter, and we never *go* there because of the Gulper . . ."

"The Gulper?" said both children at once.

"Oh, that's what my brother calls the treacherous spot I was warning you about. It lies somewhere toward the middle of the swamp, well away from shore, thank fortune (or what used to be shore), and we're never certain exactly where it will be. (Of course it's my own belief that there's more than one Gulper; I don't see how a bog could travel, do you?)"

"What ever happened to the lake, though?" said Julian.

"We think it was when they built the dam at Corinth in nineteen-hundred-and-three. Tarrigo just began to dwindle away and away until in nineteen-hundred-and-six it was all gone! Nothing was left but mud, mud, mud! . . . Oh, I cried when I heard it, even though I was grown and married by then. . . .

"Well, you can imagine what happened after that. The houses were worthless. Who'd want houses facing on a great mud-flat? Most of the families had moved away anyhow when they saw what was happening to Tarrigo, and the rest moved afterwards. These old summer houses just stood here, fading and rotting, and nobody used them but the rats and wasps and chimney swifts. Tramps came through from time to time, and hunters in the fall. They plundered and broke things and wrote on the walls. . . . But they never got into the Big House; no they did not! Nor into Villa Caprice, either!"

"Villa Caprice?" said Portia.

"Oh, yes." Mrs. Cheever laughed a little and shook her head. "That was what Mrs. Brace-Gideon called her place. In those days it was thought elegant to give names to houses. Mr. Tuckertown, for instance, being Southern and romantic, named *his* house Bellemere, and he nearly died when it was brought to his attention that that name—pronounced a little differently—means 'mother-in-law' in the French language, *particularly* as his mother-in-law did live with them and was a very strong-minded lady and a close friend of Mrs. Brace-Gideon's. Now Mrs. Brace-*Gideon's* house didn't put you in mind of a caprice at all; no it did not. It was a big stout building with cobblestone pillars; and Mrs. Brace-Gideon was a big stout woman with, you might say, a cobblestone character. She had a deep manly voice and a dark red face. She was rich, and careful about it. Let's see, where was I? . . .

"The houses that no one broke into—yes. Well, so Papa and Mrs. Brace-Gideon (*especially* Mrs. Brace-Gideon) were very conscientious and careful about locking up their houses because they'd left everything in them. There was no room for the furniture in their city houses, and to keep it all here was cheaper and easier than storing it. So they double-boarded up the windows and double-locked and bolted and boarded up the doors till not even one field mouse could have squeezed its way in! They thought, of course—Papa and Mrs. Brace-Gideon—that the time would come when they'd take their furniture away and use it somewhere else. But you never know, do you? Papa and Mama both died in the same year, nineteen-hundred-and-seven, and Mrs. Brace-Gideon perished in the San Francisco earthquake. I'm sorry to say that my brother is of the opinion that only a cataclysm of nature *could* have done for Mrs. Brace-Gideon."

"And what happened to Villa Caprice?" Portia enquired.

"Still, as far as I know, untouched," said Mrs. Cheever solemnly. "No relatives. No heirs. No caretaker; she would not pay the money to maintain one. She built her house away from these others to have it more grand and particular, I suppose. And what happened was that the woods came and captured it! The hedges are tree-high by now and all bound up with honeysuckle and poison ivy and wild grape—"

"Something like the story of Sleeping Beauty," said Portia.

"Something like the story of Rip Van Winkle," said Julian.

"Yes, except that nothing sleeps inside but furniture, and that's probably gone to pieces by now. *Time* gets into anything; yes, indeed it does; and weather helps it. And then the Boston ivy that was planted sixty years ago has crawled all over the house till it looks as if it had been knitted into a huge afghan. Owls live in the porch. . . . *I* don't like the place. . . ." The old lady gave a little shudder. "I don't mind these old house-wrecks at the edge of Gone-Away, but that Villa Caprice all shut up in the woods. . . . I don't know why, but *that* one gives me the creeps!"

"I'd like to know," said Julian hesitantly. "If you don't mind my asking, ma'am, what I'd like to know is how you happen to be here still?"

"I came back. I was gone for years. When my husband died, I found I had no money, or almost none, and I didn't know what in the world to do! And then I thought there's still the house at Tarrigo; I can go and live in that! I'd had enough of the world, anyway. My brother Pindar and I were all that was left of the family, and Pindar, who had fallen on hard times, decided he'd had enough of the world, too. So one summer morning, long ago, we fought our way through weeds and mosquitoes to the Big House. And do you know Papa had closed it up so well that, even with the key, it took us a day and a half to get in! At night we camped in this house, and when we *did* get inside the Big House, we found that though nobody else had been able to, the weather had. The attic ceiling was full of holes, and one chimney was gone. But the downstairs floors were still protected, and hardly anything was spoiled.

" 'But we can't live here,' my brother said. 'Too many leaks and too many ghosts'; and so, since we each value privacy, I chose a house at this end of the settlement and he

45

chose one at the other. We fixed them up with furniture from the Big House. I got most of it (my brother is not partial to furniture), and I thought I'll never want for a thing. I'll never need to see another town or buy another dress. Why, there were chests and cupboards full of Mama's old summer dresses and coats, and my sisters had left all theirs behind when they got married and had their new trousseaux. I never grew stout, thank fortune, and there are still dresses that I've never worn."

"But what about provisions?" Julian said. "Food and—uh—shoelaces, and things?"

"Shoelaces, for heaven's sake," said Portia.

"Well, my brother still has the Machine. . . ."

"Machine?" inquired Julian in a polite, puzzled tone.

"Automobile. Motor car. Car. I guess nowadays you call them all cars. Once a month my brother Pindar drives to Pork Ferry to get the things we need and have his hair cut. But I *never* go; no, indeed I do not. And I never will. Oh! Why, children! I haven't offered you a thing to eat or drink! Come into the kitchen and have a drop of cherry-mead. But first let me summon my brother."

Following her, and of course Julian, from the sitting room, Portia thought that she had never heard anyone use the word "summon" before.

"MY BROTHER PINDAR"

In the hall Mrs. Cheever turned toward the front door, Julian and Portia at her heels. Beyond her, through the screen, they could see the softly waving lake of reeds, now half in shadow. The pampas plumes were lighted by the slanting sun, so that they looked like golden feathers. Golden insects danced above them.

"I think we ought to start home," Julian said. "The sun looks late."

"Oh, no, wait a minute, now, do. We'll just have a sip of cherry-mead, and then my brother Pindar will show you the safe way home."

On a hook near the door, hanging by a thong, there was a large whorled sea-shell. Mrs. Cheever took it down, opened the screen door, leaned out, and raised the shell to her lips. When she blew into it, there came a great sad sound like the calling of a lost cow. She lowered the shell and appeared to be listening; in a moment another sad cow responded.

"Yes, he's there. He's coming." Mrs. Cheever twanged the screen door shut and returned the shell to its hook. "Papa and Mr. Tuckertown each had one of these to call their children home from the lake or wherever they were. We always knew which shell was calling by the difference in tone; Pindar's (that was Mr. Tuckertown's) is slightly deeper and more mournful. Real cows have been known to answer. Whenever I hear it, I'm taken right back to those times. Oh, lights on the water; all these big houses lighted up and people waiting for us to come home! And the smell of supper coming across the lake to meet us . . . and the sound of Clay Delaney's mandolin. . . . A long time ago. . . . Well, that's how it is. Now *this* is my kitchen."

She pushed open an old green baize door, soft and moth-eaten. They passed through a pantry, with shelves full of dishes, to a large, light room. After the heavy traffic in the parlor the kitchen seemed bare and almost austere. The walls were whitewashed, and on the floor an ancient linoleum had been worn away as natural things like stone or wood are worn away; here and there gone altogether, here and there a patch of faded stars and hexagons still clinging smoothly to the old clean boards. A coal range stood near the back door, crackling inside itself. Monarch was its name. It was old, too. Everything in the kitchen was old: the mended mosquito netting at the windows, the scrubbed deal table, the pots and pans. On a bracket-shelf a flock of kerosene lamps was roosting, arranged according to size, from a vase-shaped giant down to one no bigger than a tea-cup that wore on its chimney a sort of Russian halo made of tin.

"Oh, Minnie!" called a voice out-of-doors.

"There he is. I wish he wouldn't call me Minnie," said Mrs. Cheever, opening the door and stepping out on the back stoop to meet her brother. Portia and Julian stepped out, too, and saw, marching briskly toward them and knocking at daisies with a cane, an elderly and dapper gentleman. The reddish-pink of his face was accentuated by a white beard and mustache. His eyebrows were black; his eyes were sharp and blue. He wore a broad-brimmed felt hat, a tweed jacket, and blue jeans tucked into the tops of very high-laced walking boots. There was a coreopsis flower in his buttonhole. He had an air of style and elegance.

"What-ho, Minnie," called he, and his voice had an air of style and elegance, too. "Is it our good fortune to have visitors?"

"I wish you wouldn't call me Minnie," said his sister. "And you can see perfectly well that we have visitors. Very nice ones, too. Children, this is my brother Mr. Pindar Payton. And Pin, these—what did you say your names were, children?"

When they told her, Mr. Payton shook their hands warmly. "Well, this is a nice surprise," said he. "The last caller we had was a strayed mule."

"Come in and have a glass of mead," said Mrs. Cheever. "Just think, Pin, these two children came *through* the swamp to get here. I want you to show them the safe way out; they live back over Priory Ridge, between Attica and Pork Ferry."

"That's a good piece of a walk," said Mr. Payton. "About six miles, I'd judge it, when you come that way. Maybe seven."

He removed his broad hat and smoothed back his white waving hair, smoothed out the two small wings of his mustache, smoothed down his beard. Maybe he's a little vain, thought Portia, but she didn't blame him. He was a very nice-looking pink-and-white man.

They sat down at the long deal table by the window. Julian began unloading himself; hanging the camera on one corner of the back of his chair, the field glasses and the creel on the other. He propped his butterfly net against the wall and, as he sat down, placed the killing jar on the table before him.

"Jule, I don't think a cyanide jar belongs on *any* kitchen table—" Portia began virtuously, but Mr. Payton suddenly picked up the jar and looked into it.

"Aha. *Oeneis jutta;* nice specimen. Very nice," he said. "Congratulations."

Julian leaped to his feet; he looked as if lights were flashing off and on inside him. "You mean you *know*, sir? You know about *butterflies?*"

"Only swamp-and-bog varieties, I'm afraid. I'm a swamp-and-bog entomologist; strictly amateur."

"I never met *any* kind of an entomologist," Julian said. "Only me, and I don't know anything except what I read, and I can't pronounce any of the names right. Gee, am I ever glad we got lost!"

"Me, too," said Portia.

"Me, too," said Mrs. Cheever, as she put a tray down on the table. There was a decanter on it, as dark red as the garnets they had found, and four little fancy glasses, none alike, though each was stamped with silver letters that said: Chicago World's Fair, 1893. Mrs. Cheever poured the dark liquid carefully into the little glasses and handed one to each of them.

"This is made from wild chokecherries and honey; my brother keeps bees."

"I keep goats, too," said her brother, "but they don't contribute to the mead." He raised his little glass. "To a growing friendship," he said.

They all raised their glasses. Portia, watching Julian, saw that this was what they were supposed to do; and then, still watching him, she took a sip when he did.

The cherry-mead tasted like a swallow of sweet fire. It made her eyes water. But the second sip was easier.

"It has a flavor like cough drops," Portia said. "*Good* cough drops, I mean."

"Oh, it's excellent for a cough; my brother Pindar lives on it all winter," agreed Mrs. Cheever. She set a plate of cookies on the table. "Made with angelica root," she said. "It grows wild near the swamp."

"We use what we can from the swamp and the bogs," said Mr. Payton. "There's a lot of good to be found in them."

"Yes, that's what we decided," said Mrs. Cheever, nodding her head with its little sailing bow. "If we're going to be saddled with swamps and bogs for the rest of our days, we thought, well then let's find out what those things are good for, what they have to offer. Oh, yes. I tell you we were pleased, to start off with; *we'd* come back to Tarrigo —or Gone-Away—still somehow expecting to find a sea of mud. And when we found this nice green swamp, these nice green millions of reeds instead, why, they were so much better than the mud that we thought it was all just beautiful. And it *is* beautiful in an odd way, but you have to learn how to see it."

"How about those man-eating mosquitoes though, brother?" inquired Julian, lapsing into his family manners for a moment and scratching at his bitten shinbones. Portia, in sympathy, began scratching at her elbow. (An elbow is a terrible place to have a mosquito bite.)

"Oh, they wearied of us after a while," said Mr. Payton. "Time came when we were an old story to them, and they wouldn't bother to bite any more."

"Now, Pin, you know full well it was because of my Anti-Pest Decoction. I experimented," she explained to the children. "I boiled poison roots and pennyroyal and horse balm and anything else I could think of; I tried out different combinations till at last I struck one that caused any approaching mosquito to change its mind—"

"I was the proving ground," said Mr. Payton, helping himself to a little more mead. "I wonder how many human beings have voluntarily rubbed their skins with a solution of boiled skunk cabbage and wild garlic. (That particular one seemed to fascinate the mosquitoes, they visited me in conventions.) But it was all in a good cause. Minnie's A.P. Decoction really did the trick."

"I wish you wouldn't call me Minnie," said Mrs. Cheever absently. "Yes, my brother said that if we bottled and sold it, we could make a fortune. But I said *fortune,* for pity's sake; *money* coming in, *folks* coming in, why we'd have to change our ways, wear up-to-date clothes, and write business letters and all! No thank *you,* I said. I like my swamp. I like my life; what Pindar calls my 'hermitude.'"

"And she was quite right," said Mr. Payton. "Our life suits us; we want no change. Except that it would be a pleasure to have callers like yourselves drop in oftener."

"Thank you, sir," said Julian, courtly once more. "But

now I'm afraid we really must be going." He began hanging his possessions onto himself again. This time Portia was given the butterfly net to carry; he would not trust her with the precious jar.

Portia did not want to leave. "I've had a lovely time," she said, shaking Mrs. Cheever's hand regretfully. She even dropped a curtsy, a tribute of deference that she considered idiotic and usually managed to forget; but Julian's good manners were infectious.

"Will you come again?" said Mrs. Cheever.

"Would tomorrow be too soon?" asked Julian.

"Tomorrow would be exactly right. I'll show you my bog garden if the day is good."

As they left the house, the old screen-door tingled softly behind them. Somewhere a mourning dove was cooing and cooing; it had an evening sound.

"Golly, it *is* late," Julian said. "It'll take us hours to get home!"

"No, I know a quicker route. Follow me," said Mr. Pindar Payton. He trotted ahead of them past the old houses. Very old they looked in the late afternoon light; doors gaped, showing blackness beyond; jags of window glass flickered like fire. Swifts circled the chimneys.

"That one's mine," said their leader, gesturing toward the last house at the far end of the settlement. It was almost as run-down as the rest, though neater. There were chickens strolling about there, too; and they saw a healthy vegetable garden with bean wigwams in it. Beyond, near the woods, there was a series of what seemed to be rather untidy wooden boxes set up on props.

"Hives," explained Mr. Payton. "Apartment houses for bees. Show you tomorrow."

As they rounded the far end of the swamp, Portia noticed the dark tuft at its center, which must, she thought, be Craneycrow.

53

"That's Craneycrow Island," said Mr. Payton as if her thoughts had spoken. "Must be sixty years since I've set foot on it. Tarquin Tuckertown and I camped out there once but—"

"Tarquin! Did you say Tarquin, sir?" cried Julian.

"Why, yes," said Mr. Payton, stopping and turning to look at him. "I suppose it *is* a fairly unusual name."

"'Tarquin et Pindar,'" chanted Julian, watching Mr. Payton. "'Lapis Philosophorum.' The something-or-other of July, 1891."

"I beg your pardon?" For a moment their new friend looked gravely alarmed. Then his face cleared, and he laughed. "Well, by Jupiter! The stone. The philosopher's stone! Well, by Jove. Is it still there? You found it?"

"This very day," said Portia.

"And I skinned some moss off the top of it when we were looking for garnets, and there were the words," Julian explained. "We wondered who'd put them there, and why."

"By Jupiter! By Jove! There *were* garnets in the rock. I recollect. Those words were carved the summer that Tark and I—but, no, we'll save the story for another time. Too late today. Now then, Julian, do you see that opening in the woods?"

"The place that looks like a road?"

"Yes, and for the very good reason that it was a road once: a wagon road over the ridge. . . . It's overgrown, now, but you can still follow it. You'll come out on Creston Turnpike, but the hazel bushes have grown high at that end. Mark them well. From the turnpike the old wagon road is completely hidden; wouldn't easily find it again yourself if you weren't certain of the spot. Might be a good idea to leave a marker there. On the turnpike bear left and you'll be home in fifteen minutes."

"Thank you, sir."

"Thank you, sir," said Portia.

"Oh, and another thing," warned Mr. Payton. "On the turnpike watch out for the *machines*. They go by as if they're late for Judgment Day!"

"We will! Good-by."

"Good-by."

"Good-by."

Portia and Julian toiled up the stoney old road; up and up and up, then across the brambled ridge, and down the other side. Loose stones rolled from under their feet and briars caught at their clothes. High up, the sun still slanted through the treetops, but down below the air felt damp and cool. Already they could hear the swish of cars along the turnpike. Julian's jingling had a weary sound, and Portia thought she might be growing a blister on her heel.

"I liked today," Julian said. "I liked *them*."

"I loved them," said Portia.

"I was just thinking, though," Julian continued. Then he stopped, examined a black birch beside the rutted path, and with great care and deliberation selected a twig to chew. Portia picked one, too, and bit it to taste its wintergreen flavor.

"Thinking *what*, for heaven's sake?" she demanded finally, just as he wanted her to.

"I was thinking that maybe it might be a good idea to keep this—them—the swamp and the old dumps of houses —everything—a secret for a while. Not mention it to any-one. Just to avoid complications and things."

"Yes! Let's have it a secret for a while. I don't see why not, do you?" Portia felt a faint doubt, but was able to smother this quite comfortably and quickly.

"We won't lie about it or anything, I mean; just sort of keep quiet about it. Right?"

"Right," said Portia.

5

THE SECOND TIME

They were not able to return to Gone-Away the next day until the afternoon. Julian had to mow the lawn in the morning, and Aunt Hilda needed Portia's help with the weeding. But the children didn't mind; home was a good, interesting place, the weather was perfect, and they had their secret to look forward to. The puppies had been brought out-of-doors to roll and tumble on the grass. They staggered about, their eyes sun-dazzled and their tongues hanging out. The great feathered peonies loomed over them like palm trees. Katy moved among her children with a worried, possessive air. One of them kept wandering away by himself, and she would go after him, take him up by the loose skin at the back of his neck, and bring him back where he belonged.

"We could call that one Gulliver," Portia suggested, "because he's always traveling."

"Excellent," said Aunt Hilda. "It suits him."

"Aunt Hilda, is this a weed I'm pulling?"

"Oh, no, heavens, that's a delphinium! I don't think you've disturbed it much, though; just press the earth back firmly. Now this beastly little thing with the fat stems *is* a weed. So is this one with the fancy leaves that looks as if it ought to be a flower."

The sun was warm, but a soft wind stirred among the

trees as though it were stroking and turning the wealth of new leaves, counting them over. Julian's lawn mower made a sound of metal snoring back and forth across the lawn, and the little boys in their hollow tree were just as shrill as the shrill blue-jays. (Davey Gayson had arrived at seven o'clock that morning, sitting patiently on the kitchen doorstep, clicking his empty cap-pistol until the family came down for breakfast.)

Just now they were preparing to blast off again.

"Turn the nose east, path vertical," ordered Foster.

"What do you mean, vertical?" said Davey.

"Straight up, of course. We have to use the speed of the earth's rotation, don't we? We're going to the place the moon will be four days from now, aren't we?"

"I guess so," said Davey.

"My soul, the things children know these days—" sighed Aunt Hilda.

"And Foster can't really read yet," said Portia. "Only 'yow!' and 'wham!' and 'bop!' Comic-book words. He can read all *those*."

In the huge swinging maple tree the oriole stopped his work from time to time and sang. The house wrens sang, too, but their song seemed more in the nature of conversation, and in the woods a certain red cardinal sounded like a little bottle being filled up, up, up with some clear liquid.

"If you could just hold onto it," said Portia, sitting back on the warm grass. Her knees were stiff from kneeling.

"Onto what? The weather?" Aunt Hilda sat back on the grass, too, and pushed her tumbled hair away from her brow with the back of her muddy hand. She was a very pretty woman.

"The weather, partly, but mostly the time. June like this, and everything starting to be. Summer starting to be. Everything just exactly *right*."

"But if it were this way every day, all the time, we'd get

too used to it. We'd *toughen* to it," said Aunt Hilda. "People do. It's just because it doesn't and can't last that a day like this is so wonderful."

"Good things must have comparers, I suppose," said Portia. "Or how would we know how good they are?"

"Exactly!" Aunt Hilda went back to her weeding; and after a minute Portia did, too.

"But I bet *I'd* know it was good even if it lasted forever," she said. She felt a sudden stab of pleasure at the thought of Gone-Away and wished that she could tell her aunt about it, but knew she must not break her promise to Julian.

Foster and Davey were tired of the hollow tree. They erupted from it suddenly and tore around and around the lawn. Katy forgot her children and tore with them.

"We're orbital space stations," shouted Foster, flashing by. "Katy's one, too!"

After lunch (Davey departed to eat his with greatest reluctance and returned from it still chewing), Portia and Julian raced through the dishwashing and started on their way.

It was hot walking along the turnpike; the cars that zipped by left a hot smell behind them. Portia and Julian were glad when they came to the long bank of hazel bushes. The evening before they had been puzzled as to what to leave for a marker. Julian had solved the problem by removing his sneaker, peeling off one of his red socks, grubby with bog water, and tying it to a twig.

"But what will your mother say?"

"She'll never miss it. Or if she does, she won't worry. Things are always happening to my socks. One's always going off someplace. *I* don't know why."

They had no difficulty locating the sock now and, pushing their way through the scratchy thicket, were soon on their way up the old rough road. Julian as usual was draped with equipment, but today his jingling sounded brisk, and

Portia skipped and bounced beside him with no thought of blisters.

As they came down the far side of the ridge, they looked with pleasure at the peculiar scene before them: Craney-crow riding like a dark secret vessel on its lake of reeds, all rippling and floating under the summer wind; the arc of ruined houses with their broken windows and tipped towers; and beyond those the encroaching woods.

"I see Mr. Pindar Payton. See? Out there by the bee-hives," said Julian.

The sight of him caused them both to break into a canter. "Hi, Mr. Payton!" shouted Julian, as they approached. The old gentleman straightened up, smiling, and removed his broad hat and waved it. Wind ruffled his white hair.

"Welcome! Welcome!" he said when they reached him, red-cheeked and panting. "You look hot. Come in and have a drink of water."

He led them to his door; (there was a thread-spool to turn instead of a knob, they noticed); and as he opened it, Mr. Payton stood aside to let Portia enter first. Portia looked at Julian and lifted the corner of her lip as she went by him.

"This is my living room," said their host. "Not much in it, not much needed. Only use two rooms of the house myself. Hornets occupy the attic. Rest is empty."

His living room was nothing in the world like Mrs. Cheever's. There was a horsehair sofa (raveling), a neat narrow bed, two or three chairs, a table with a radio and an oil lamp on it, and a potbellied stove, cold now, supporting a washstand pitcher full of German iris. Books were neatly piled in chimney-stacks against the wall, and the only adornment *on* the wall was a large piece of tacked-up wrapping paper with Latin words printed on it.

"And here's the kitchen; my real living-room," said Mr. Payton, opening another door. "Hornets make it advisable to live hermetically sealed in summer."

"But couldn't you get rid of them, sir? DDT, or something?"

"Tell you the truth I wouldn't want to. I like the feeling of all that coming and going, all that business being carried on upstairs. They're there, but I don't have to know 'em. Like living in a hotel."

The kitchen was big. The walls were white here, too, but the floor was painted a cheerful red. The black range looked like Mrs. Cheever's Monarch but was, if anything, even larger and fancier. Its name was Sultana. On the kitchen walls were several cases of mounted butterflies and moths, an old-fashioned hexagonal clock with a pendulum, and a grocery-store calendar with a picture on it of a girl (a grown-up girl) swinging.

Mr. Payton had a big deal table like his sister's, and a smaller table with a set of kitchen chairs, and two real sitting chairs: a rocker, and an armchair with stuffing bursting out of it. Asleep in the armchair was an unusually large, cushiony striped cat, fast asleep.

"That's Fatly," Mr. Payton said.

"Fatly? Is that his name?"

"It is."

Hearing his name, the cat woke up. He looked at them with eyes the color of melted butter and pushed out one paw in a stretch.

"Well, it suits him now," said Portia, the authority on names. "But what about when he was a little tiny kitten?"

"Ah, but I didn't know him then. He came into my life as a cat of mature years. One winter night, three years ago, I heard him calling out-of-doors. Terrible night. Snow driving down. Wind howling in such a way that at first I thought Fatly's cries were part of it. And then the storm lulled for a moment but Fatly did not; and I recognized the sound as being of true cat origin, opened the door and in he walked, fat but half-frozen, twitching the snow off his ears. He settled right down to a dish of tuna fish, without objection, and afterwards turned on his purr. Sounded like a jackhammer. Next day he brought a dead rat and laid it on my doorstep. Gesture of gratitude; I think he expected me to eat it."

Cats, like most children, do not care to hear themselves discussed. Fatly now rose to his full height, arched himself like a croquet wicket, and dropped heavily to the floor. He stalked from the room, his collar-bell tinkling.

"Bell's to warn the birds," Mr. Payton explained. "But unfortunately Fatly knows how to muffle it with his chin. A cat of ingenuity. Of native intelligence. A shrewd cat."

As he spoke, Mr. Payton was wielding the arm of a tall pump that had its abode at the end of an iron sink. *Hee*-haw, *hee*-haw, brayed the pump, and presently water spouted forth, cold and clear. Mr. Payton filled two rose-trimmed teacups and handed one to each child.

"That's the best water I ever tasted in my life," said Julian, eloquently wiping off his mouth with his sleeve.

"Now come out and view the rest of the estate," said Mr. Payton, clapping on his hat. Again he held the door open for Portia. I wonder if he had manners like that when he was a kid, thought Julian. Gosh. Probably not, though.

First they walked around the vegetable garden and admired it. It was perfect; the rows looked as if they had been laid down by the yard, they were so even. Bees hummed in the flowering bean-wigwams. The garden was fenced round with chicken wire.

"Rabbits," explained their host. "Ground hogs. Even deer out of the woods, to say nothing of my own livestock. Everybody's hungry. But I don't let 'em starve. Over here, you see, is my rabbit garden. No fence. Lettuce just the same as mine. Carrots. Nice green peas. Makes sense, doesn't it? Plenty for all. And I plant millet and sunflowers for the birds."

"Ma-a-a-a!" cried a voice in the distance. It had a very querulous sound.

"Who's that?" said Portia, startled.

"Just Florence," replied Mr. Payton. "Come, I'll show you." They followed him along a path that led to a large enclosure, well away from the house. It was informally fenced about with old doors, lengths of picket fence, boards, and chicken wire. The gate was an ancient bedspring. In the enclosure, grazing in the roving shade, was a family of goats.

"*They* are not welcome in my rabbit garden," said Mr. Payton. "But now and then they break out just the same. The billy goat's called Uncle Sam. No disrespect intended. No indeed. Just something about the way he wears his beard—well, he just seemed to *require* the name."

"The nanny is named Florence because she reminds me of a cousin I used to have. Not the way she looks. The way she sounds."

"Ma-a-a-a," complained Florence.

"*Just* the way my cousin used to sound when she was calling her mother," mused Mr. Payton. "She was always calling her mother. A very demanding child. Spoiled. Bad case of adenoids."

"Ma-a-a-a," said Uncle Sam, two tones deeper and dryer.

Uncle Sam and Florence had two kids; beautiful little soft-eared creatures, dainty as gazelles. "They haven't any names, though. I just call them both Junior. They still drink milk out of a bottle. Would you like to feed them later?"

"I'd love to!" said Portia.

Mr. Payton unfastened the bedspring gate and opened it. "You may come out for a moment, babies." Out skipped the kids; Portia was immediately on her knees beside them.

"Ma-a-a-a!" said Uncle Sam.

"Not you, you old rascal," said Mr. Payton, fastening the bedspring into place. Uncle Sam peered through the wires. He had a crafty face; the pupil of each of his pale eyes was shaped like the slot in a piggy bank. He smelled

very strongly of goat. Mr. Payton reached in and scratched the boney forehead between the curved-back horns.

Suddenly they heard another sound: the soft, melodious mooing of a conch shell.

"My sister wants company, I imagine," said Mr. Payton. "Well, well, I mustn't be selfish. Let's go pay her a visit, but first," he said, noticing that his guests had begun to slap themselves, "we'll stop at my house so that you can put on some A.P. Decoction. Come, Juniors, back into the pen with you."

The decoction, they soon discovered, had a very assertive, difficult smell. But as Mr. Payton had said, it did the trick, and after a while one's nose became resigned.

The reeds were shimmering and bending to the right of them as they walked the narrow path in single file. To the left stood the old houses. As they passed each one, Mr. Payton pointed to it with his cane and named the family who had owned it.

"That one belonged to the Delaneys; a big family. Came from Cedar Rapids. Musical. Had a pianola. And the one we're coming to belonged to the Vogelharts. Beer money. Nine children. A very fat family. And the one beyond with all the caved-in porches is Bellemere; belonged to our best friends, the Tuckertowns. 'Mother-in-law Mansion,' as poor Mr. Tuckertown had to hear it called. . . ."

What had once been lawns were now wild, weedy meadows; hedges, once neatly trimmed, had grown into trees. Here and there iris grew in patches, and so did peonies and Oriental poppies; and roses, unpruned for generations, still bloomed on broken fences, spreading their long tentacles over the grass, like flowered shawls.

"Now *that* house, set back, was ours: the Big House. Mighty gone to seed . . ."

All the houses were gone to seed, and one of them had collapsed entirely. It lay, a mountain of rubble, draped in wild cucumber vines. "That belonged to the Castle family. They called it The Castle Castle, which we thought very witty when we were young. . . . Ah, Minnie, good afternoon!"

Mrs. Cheever, coming to meet them, was wearing a pink blouse with leg-of-mutton sleeves; a long dark skirt with an apron over it; and a bell-shaped Panama hat tied on with a veil. She looked peculiar but nice.

"I'm happy to see you again, children! Yes, indeed I am!" she cried. "Children are such valuable creatures, aren't they, Pin?"

"Nice ones are."

"All of them are!" declared Mrs. Cheever. "If they're nice, you notice it more, though. Would you care to see my bog garden, Portia? Julian? Good; the arethusas are in bloom. And then we'll go back to my house and have a little refreshment. I've baked a cake."

Julian restrained himself from asking what kind of cake, but in his heart was the passionate hope that it was chocolate.

"Oh, but you will get your feet wet!" cried Mrs. Cheever at the swamp's edge. "I am wearing overshoes."

"Don't give it a thought, ma'am," said Julian, sitting down and starting to unlace his Keds. "Barefoot's the answer." Portia followed suit.

"As for me, I believe I'll wait in your house, Minnie, and enjoy a little glass of mead," said her brother. As he departed he was singing:

"Has anybody here seen Kelly?
Kelly of the emerald isle. . . ."

Mrs. Cheever led the way. The water was warm and squelchy under the children's bare feet. Portia thought about snakes, then decided not to think about them. Redwinged blackbirds seemed to be everywhere, cluck-clucking at these foreigners, or swinging like ornaments on the tops of the reeds, whistling.

"But, Mrs. Cheever," said Julian, sounding rather nervous. "What about this—this Gulper?"

"Oh, that's far out—or *they* are—near Craneycrow somewhere. This part is perfectly safe."

Presently the reeds thinned and grew scarce. They saw a dead tree, weather-silvered, standing in a clear space. A nest of sticks was clutched in one of its angular bleached boughs.

"That tree marks the entrance to the bog," said Mrs. Cheever. "You can tell that we are in a true bog now, you see, because of all the spagnum moss."

The moss was the softest thing that Portia had ever stepped on. "Like walking on wet mink," she said dreamily.

"Mink shmink," scoffed Julian. "Better than that; like walking on an acre of whipped cream."

The spagnum grew in silver-green cushions; it oozed water at every step, dark water the color of strong tea that had a rich delicious smell.

"I bet this is the way the earth smelled in prehistoric days," observed Julian, sniffing.

"Well, nobody's going to contradict you," said Portia. (She had just stubbed her toe on a root.)

"Exactly like this, I bet," persisted Julian. "But of course there probably would have been a smell of dinosaurs, too. I wonder what that was like? Fish, maybe?"

"More like wet raincoats, I should think," said Portia. "Thousands and thousands of wet raincoats and galoshes."

Beyond a wide cluster of sheep laurel, all specked with flowers, was the bog garden. They had never seen a garden like it; nothing was planted in a bed. It looked as though it had been the work of nature alone. By dark still pools grew leathery pitcher-plants, whose urn-shaped leaves held water and drowned insects, and whose wine-colored flowers were like the umbrellas of Siamese kings.

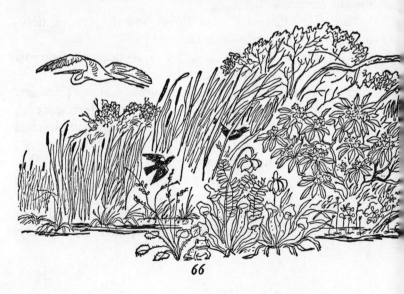

"Those plants are meat-eaters," said Mrs. Cheever. "And so is this little one, the sundew."

Portia bent over to examine it. The plant had round flat leaves, each edged with a red honey-beaded fringe, useful for snaring gnats. Here other sorts of moss were growing: a kind that resembled a miniature pine forest, and another that made her think of multitudes of tiny festival lanterns carried on sticks.

"But do look at my arethusas. I am so proud of them," pleaded Mrs. Cheever.

They were lovely flowers, the arethusas, each one solitary, leafless, its pink blossom eared like a little fox.

"Oh, they're so delicate," said Mrs. Cheever tenderly. "Rare, too. Every spring I fear they won't come up again. And yet they do, thank fortune. They are orchids—"

"Goodness, I thought orchids were just florist flowers. *Trained* flowers. I never thought about them being wild."

"There are many kinds, though. Here's one called snake-mouth, and over there the grass pink. Later on there will be others. Oh, you must come often during the summer and see—" Mrs. Cheever turned, smiling at Portia. "I never realized how much I wanted an audience for this garden!"

"Well, it's beautiful. But how do you get them all to grow where you want them to?"

"The orchids are the difficult ones. I roam the bogs, of course, and when I find a plant in flower, I mark it with a stake. (Pindar always cuts me some and paints them red so I can find them later.) I never *touch* the plant till frost has come, and then I dig up the frozen sod beside each marker (praying that the bulb is in it) and plant it in my own bog garden. Sometimes the orchids don't come up, but usually they do. My brother says I have a real bog-thumb."

Julian, who was slopping about some distance away, was heard to say: "Doggone it!"

"Why, what's the matter?"

"Heck! I just saw a butterfly I can't pronounce that I need! And I left my equipment at Mr. Payton's house. Doggone it!" repeated Julian with feeling.

"That little copper-colored thing? You'll see it often here; so you must come often," Mrs. Cheever said comfortingly.

"Oh, we plan to come every day, practically," Portia assured her.

Across the reed-tops came the sound of a conch shell. "Pin's getting hungry, children. Come along," said Mrs. Cheever.

The hem of her dark skirt was soaking wet, but she didn't seem to mind. "Old people are supposed to suffer from the damp," she observed, her wet skirt slapping at her heels. "But it's my belief that what they *need* is dampness.

My brother and I hardly know the *meaning* of the word rheumatism. No, indeed, we do not!"

Puffs of midges smoked in the air; mosquitoes, tuned like peevish violins, approached and departed, disheartened by the fumes of the A.P. Decoction. A heron rose with an awkward noise and flapped away, his legs trailing. . . .

Mrs. Cheever's kitchen was calm and cool. Mr. Payton, in a chair by the window, was reading a very old newspaper. "Old news is more soothing to read about," he said. "You know that you lived through it all right."

On the table, where four places were set, there was a chocolate cake under a glass bell. Julian noted with pleasure (so did Portia) that it was a triple-decker, with the frosting laid on one inch thick.

"It's my belief that a fudge cake should be *built*," Mrs. Cheever said, "strong and thick, the way the Mexicans build adobe houses. You may wash your hands here at the pump, children, and I suggest you do so. A.P. Decoction has a fearful flavor."

When they were seated at the table drinking tea and eating the splendid cake, Julian remembered what he had wanted to find out about.

"Sir," he said respectfully to Mr. Payton, "do you think you could tell us now, please, about the philosopher's stone?"

"Aha," said Mr. Payton, looking pleased. He wiped his mustache delicately with a damask napkin. "Just wait till I light up my pipe—Minnie, may I light my pipe?—and I'll be glad to!"

6

THE KNIFE AND THE BUTTONHOOK

"Now this took place a long, long time ago," said Mr. Payton. Then he puff-puffed on his pipe, sucked in the smoke, watched to see that the tobacco was safely alight, and continued. "A very long time ago. Shortly after the extinction of the dinosaurs it was."

(Well, of course he doesn't really mean it was as long ago as that, thought Portia.)

"Tarrigo was a busy little summer colony then, busy and well-to-do. All the houses were occupied, and all of them, except Mrs. Brace-Gideon's, had children in them. Hers had pug dogs and summer cats. Gardens were nicely cared for, lawns mowed; everybody had plenty of help. You could always hear an ice-cream freezer being cranked away on a back porch, tennis balls thumping, croquet balls knocking, waves slapping. Seems like that, doesn't it, Min?"

"Yes, yes." Mrs. Cheever stirred her tea, smiling at memory. "And it seems as if all the days were sunny, and each one longer than a week."

"Our best friends were the Tuckertowns. They had five children. Tarquin was the eldest boy—we called him Tark —and though he was three years older than I was, we were close friends. His sister Baby-Belle was Minnie's best friend."

"Calpurnia was her real name, I recollect," said Mrs. Cheever. "But Baby-Belle was what they called her. Her elder sister was Octavia Cassandra, and the little ones were Auriella Lee and Hannibal."

"They all had heavily embroidered names," said Mr. Payton.

"Ours were no better, Pin. Think of Minnehaha Augusta and Pindar Peregrine and Persephone and Polyhymnia and Alexander Manfred Lionel. Those were our names, but everyone called us Min and Pin and Persy and Polly and Lex. But go on, Pin, I'm interrupting."

"Well, sir, Tark Tuckertown and I used to have the time of our lives those summers. We knew this countryside for miles around. We knew the sloughs where you'd catch the most chub and shiners, and the places along the river where you could pull out a catfish or a walleyed pike. And of course there was the lake to fish in, too, but we liked to roam. We knew where the caves were, and the pastures that contained mean bulls, and the farms that had the most accessible melon-patches. Oh, and arrowheads! We knew a field where you'd always find arrowheads after a rain; and a cliff where fossil fishes were set in the rock—"

"Fossil fishes!" cried Julian.

"But gone, now," said Mr. Payton regretfully. "Blasted out. Now it's part of the turnpike, and right on that site there's an Esso filling station."

"Heck," said Julian.

"And the arrowhead collecting-ground is buried in Catalpa Street under the Pork Ferry Lion's Club."

"Heck twice," said Julian.

"Well, as I say, we knew this land around here like the palms of our dirty hands. Seems as though there was always something new to find, though. The country never wore out for us."

"I know what you mean," agreed Julian.

"For instance, one day, rambling over a ridge we'd rambled over a hundred times before, we came on a clearing, and in the middle of it was a huge, round boulder—"

71

"The philosopher's stone!" said Portia and Julian with one voice.

"Yes, but it had no name at the time. Well, by Jupiter, we were thunderstruck! Here was this mammoth rock that we had missed entirely. Tark wondered if it was a meteor. 'Might have fallen out of the sky since last time we were here,' he said.

" 'With *ferns* on it?' I said to him. 'With moss on it?' For once I was smarter than he was!"

"I thought maybe it was a meteorite myself," Portia admitted. "Only for a minute, though."

"Only till I told her," said Julian.

"Well, it's a mighty odd-looking rock from any standpoint," said Mr. Payton. "So we explored around it and climbed up on it, and Tark said: 'Let's keep this thing a secret for a while. We could use it for a secret meeting place or something.' Of course I agreed. So all that summer and the next one we'd arrange to meet at the rock whenever we thought of it; and that meant that instead of just *going* to it together in a sensible, orderly manner, we'd skulk away from Tarrigo on separate routes, keeping well out of each other's way so that we could really and honestly 'meet' at the rock. It was important to us then, blessed if I know why. First thing we'd do when we got to it was climb up on it and eat whatever we'd swiped from the pantry or wheedled out of the cook. In those days we ate steadily, like cattle, and everything agreed with us. After that, we'd play whatever we wanted. Sometimes that boulder was a battleship, and sometimes it was a stockade besieged by Hurons, and now and then it was one of Hannibal's elephants that we called Tasker, for some reason. And sometimes we just lay there and chipped out garnets or watched the ants—"

"Their grandchildren still live there," said Portia. "We ate a few yesterday, by mistake."

"We must have eaten legions," said Mr. Payton. "But

they, like everything else, agreed with us. Those were good summers. But then the third summer, the third June, when all the families came back to Tarrigo, I found a change in my friend Tark. He'd been away to school in the East. I was only ten, after all, and he was thirteen; that sometimes makes a difference when you're children. He'd always been taller than I was, and added to everything else, *that* year he'd grown three inches to my one. He loomed above me, tall and thin, and made me feel fat as a woodchuck. He brought a new way of talking, too, sort of drawling and lofty, and he wore shoes all the time. Also he'd brought a friend. Now that friend's name was—let me see—I've buried it somewhere—oh, yes, his name was Edward Cleveland Bailey, the second or third or something, and he was tall and drawly, too. I never felt so left out of things before or since. One day I went around to Bellemere, fishing rod on my shoulder, worms in a can. 'Want to go fishing?' I said. And Tark was sitting on the porch railing swinging one foot. 'You call that stuff fishing? Chub? Pumpkinseeds? Bluegills?' says he. 'My word, you should go fishing in the Stream sometime. Fishing for kings. That's the life, isn't it, Ed?'

" 'What do you mean kings? What do you mean stream?' I said. 'Some stream around here?'

" 'The *Gulf* Stream, he means, of course,' says Edward Bailey. 'In the Atlantic Ocean, off the Florida coast. And by kings he means king*fish*, naturally. Great Scott.'

" 'Oh,' I said. I still didn't know what a kingfish was, but I was through asking.

" 'We went Stream-fishing in the Christmas holidays on Ed's father's yacht. That's the only kind of fishing for me,' says Tark.

" 'Yacht!' said I, in spite of myself.

" 'A yacht is a boat,' said Ed, very drawly and lofty. He was lying on his back in the hammock studying the sole of his shoe as if there was a message on it. I remember

73

it perfectly. 'A yacht is a boat,' says he. 'A boat sails on water. You can live on it if it's big enough. My father's boat is big enough. She's called the *Naiad*, and she's eighty feet long. We had a capital time aboard her, didn't we, Tark? Remember the time Curt Vanderpool took the wheel?'

"Tark began to laugh, and then they both laughed and didn't bother to explain the joke to me, and by and by I just slunk off by myself and I didn't go fishing, either. Chub didn't seem very exciting game just then. I felt lonesome—hurt; and I'd never felt that way before. Hurt me in the stomach, I recollect.

"It kept on that way, too, and after a while I left them alone. Luckily for me I had other friends, a tribe of them. Barney Delaney, for instance, was what I guess you'd call my second-best friend at Tarrigo. One day I decided to show him the boulder in the woods; I figured Tark had outgrown our secret meeting place. So one gray day after a rain, when the tennis courts were wet and the lake too cold to swim in, I said to Barney: 'I'll show you something I'll bet you never saw. It's a place. Let's take a picnic there.' Barney agreed, and pretty soon we were trudging and scratching our way among the briars and hazel bushes till we came to the clearing where the big rock was. And there, sitting on top of it eating *their* lunch were Tark Tuckertown and Edward Bailey.

" 'Come on up, Barney,' I said, climbing the rock. 'There's room up there for us, too.'

" 'No there isn't, Pin,' says Tark to me, with his mouth full. 'Little kids aren't allowed any more.'

"Little kids! That made us smart all over, Barney and me.

" 'This is the headquarters of the Philosopher's Club,' says Edward Cleveland Bailey, the second, third, or fourth. 'And you can't be a philosopher before you're thirteen. Nobody can be.'

"Well, I didn't know whether a philosopher was an animal or a fish, and certainly Barney didn't, either.

"'There's our mark, see,' says Tark, pointing with a piece of sandwich, and there, sure enough, I see words chiseled in the rock: LAPIS PHILOSOPHORUM.

"'What's that mean?' asks Barney.

"'That's for us to know and you to find out,' says Tark in a kind, gentlemanly manner.

"'And what's the lingo?' Barney persists.

"Edward Bailey, at that, took on a look of shocked disbelief. 'You mean you young ones don't know any *Latin?* In this day and age? No one can be a philosopher that doesn't know *Latin.*'

"'Those words mean that this rock is ours, not yours,' says Tark to me. 'They mean we've claimed it.'

"'Listen!' I said. 'It's mine as much as yours! We both found it the very same day, Tark Tuckertown, and you can't hog it all!'

"'But Ed and I have *claimed* it,' says Tark in a patient, let-me-keep-my-temper sort of voice. 'When you're old enough to be a philosopher, you can have a share in it, too. *Maybe* you can.'

"Well, I was ready to do something drastic: punch Tark, kick Ed, burst out crying; something. But Barney kept his head and held me back.

"'Oh, who wants to stay where they're not wanted?' says he. 'Let these fellows keep their silly pebble. Come on, Pin, I know a better place.'"

"Did he really know a better place?" Portia interrupted.

"No. He was pretending. We wound up glumly in the old Patch Corner graveyard and ate our lunch amongst the nettles and wild roses. The hurt in my stomach had come back again, but I don't recall that it impaired my appetite one particle.

"When I got home, I looked up the word 'philosopher' in the dictionary. And it said that that was a learned person who meets all the conditions of his life, bad or good, with calmness and impunity. Words to that effect. Surprised me; that wasn't the picture of Tarquin Tuckertown I had at all. Or of Ed Bailey, either. But I couldn't find *lapis philosophorum.*

"I knew where to apply, though. My father wouldn't have named his children as he did if he hadn't been something of a scholar. Persephone, Polyhymnia. All that. So that night after dinner, I went into the library where he was writing letters. 'Papa,' said I, and he held up one hand, the hand with the ring on it, and said, 'One moment, please.' Pen scratched on. I waited, watching him. A mighty fine-looking man, wasn't he, Min?"

"Oh, and the loveliest beard!" said his sister. "Pure gold. He parted it in the middle, and it flew away sideways off his chin in two directions, like two wings; and his mustache flew sideways off his upper lip like two littler wings. You don't see beards like that nowadays. No, indeed you do not!"

Mr. Payton was at work on his pipe again, lighting and coaxing it. "They need constant attention, pipes, like babies and guinea hens," he said, and sucked in the smoke. "There. Well, then, finally my father laid down his pen. 'What can I do for you, son?' he asked me.

" 'Please, sir, what is a *lapis philosophorum?*' I said.

" 'What's a *what?*' says he. Of course I didn't know how to pronounce the words, but I was a pretty good speller, and when I wrote them down, he was able to tell me. He said that in the days of antiquity it was believed by alchemists that some place there existed a stone or mineral that could change base metal, any metal, into gold or silver. 'But why do you want to know, son?' says he. 'What have you been reading?'

" 'A rock, sir,' I said, and then I told him the whole story.

" 'Well, well,' said he. 'So Tarquin Tuckertown is a philosopher now, is he? Last season he was a buckaroo, was he not? Well!'

76

"I asked my father how old you had to be before you were a philosopher, and he said: 'I don't know that I'd say thirteen was the requisite age. I've seen babies could be called philosophical. I've seen cows that could. Curry Castle's uncle, Professor Pardee, is a learned philosopher, and old Ben Gateway that rakes the drives is a natural one. Now, son, let me see your pocketknife.' That surprised me. He laid my knife on his desk beside the gold one that *he* had (present from some grateful client). 'About the same size,' he said, nodding his head. 'Sufficiently the same size. I suppose Barney has a buttonhook, has he not?'

" 'Why, I suppose so, sir,' I said, and I wondered what my father was getting at.

" 'Listen to me, son. I have a little joke in mind,' my father explained. 'Perfectly harmless, just a little joke. But you and Barney will have to practice—'

"So Barney and I prepared for the joke. Kept our ears to the ground, too, and finally one day we heard Tark and Edward Bailey planning to take a picnic to the rock.

" 'Come on, Barney,' said I. 'Not a minute to lose. Get your equipment; I'll get mine. Hurry!'

"I knew a short cut, and in no time Barney and I were scurrying through the woods; I was armed with two pocket knives and Barney with two—"

"Buttonhooks!" yelped Julian. "Was one a gold one?"

"You've guessed it!" Mr. Payton said. "One was the solid-gold one from my mother's dresser. It had been a birthday gift from Mrs. Brace-Gideon—"

"Mother never cared for it," Mrs. Cheever interrupted. "She said she'd rather have a gold *anything* than a gold buttonhook!"

"Well, it came in handy that day," said Mr. Payton. "So when we got to the boulder we climbed up on it and waited, and when Tark and Edward Bailey arrived, they found us bent over, industriously chipping out garnets: I with my own knife, Barney with his buttonhook. He used it as a

77

driver, knocking the end with a stone. Awkward. But it had to be a buttonhook, as that was the only other solid-gold article, aside from jewelry, that our house afforded.

"Oh, those fellows were outraged! 'I thought I told you young ones—' Tark begins, but I stop him.

" 'Just a minute,' I tell him, 'ju-u-st a minute. I'll go as soon as I've got this garnet out for my sister—' "

" 'But the garnets are ours, too!' yells Edward Bailey, the eighth, ninth, or tenth, mad as a bull. I saw that I'd better do my stunt before he pushed me off the rock, so I hastily performed the little sleight-of-hand trick that my father had taught me. Very useful. Very adroit. Suddenly in my hand, instead of my plain pocketknife, I held a golden one!

"I think I dissembled rather creditably. 'Gold!' I cried, gasping like a fish and goggling my eyes. 'Fellows, my knife's turned into *gold!* It's a miracle, that's what it is; a MIRACLE!'

" 'What the deuce are you howling about?' says Edward the Seventh, or whatever he was. And then he came over and looked, and his eyes goggled too, all right.

" 'Gold!' he says blankly. 'I mean it really is gold, Tark. Look at this—'

"They were so taken aback that Barney was able to exchange the ordinary buttonhook for the gold one he had in his pocket without bothering about sleight-of-hand. Then he starts shouting, too.

" 'GOLD!' he shouts. 'What's going on here? *Pin,* my buttonhook's turned golden, *too!*'

"I swear those two boys, Tarquin and Ed, looked positively scared. Positively scared.

" '*Lapis philosophorum!*' says Tark in a low, awed voice, hissing the words. 'We've found one. We've got one!'

"I looked at Barney and looked away fast. He had that bottled-up, heaving look of somebody trying not to laugh.

" 'We've made our fortunes, that's all. We'll be famous forever, that's all,' Tark was saying. Ed Bailey came back to

78

earth first. 'Hand over that knife and that buttonhook, you fellows,' he ordered. 'If *our* rock turned them into gold, it's *our* gold; nobody gave you permission—'

"'Listen, they're *our* buttonhook and knife,' said I. 'No one ever asked them to turn into gold. Use your own knives and buttonhooks—'

"But Tark was already scraping away at the surface of the rock with his penknife. He looked mad. 'It's a trick!' he said. 'This thing isn't changing at all!'

"Barney and I prepared to leave, but Barney had the last word. 'Why, fellows,' says he. '*We* were nearly an hour hacking away at that rock before the miracle happened. You have to keep *at* it.'

"The last thing we saw as we leapt off the boulder like a pair of apes was those two boys bent over working and scraping; a very pleasing sight."

"I think it was pretty mean," said Mrs. Cheever. "I call it a mean trick."

"Well, Minnie, it was *Papa's* idea," said Mr. Payton, and for one queer instant, old gentleman though he was, Portia could imagine what he had looked like as a boy.

"I think those guys deserved it," said Julian.

"Oh, *boys*," sighed Mrs. Cheever. "They all hang together."

"But what happened next?" demanded Portia. Endings never satisfied her. She wanted to go beyond them. In fairy tales when the prince and princess "lived happily ever after," she was the one who wished to know how many children they had had, what they had named them, and whether the old witch had ever put in another appearance.

"What happened next," replied Mr. Payton, looking into his pipe, which had gone out for good, "was that we lay very low, kept very quiet. We did not wish to meet the would-be alchemists for a while; and as things turned out, it had all happened toward the end of the numbered Edward

Cleveland Bailey's visit. Soon he returned to whatever superior place he'd come from, and Tark came looking for me. I was worried."

"So you should have been," said his sister firmly.

"But Tark was splendid," replied Mr. Payton. "He came to me and said: 'You fellows certainly made donkeys out of Ed and me, Pin, and we were pretty sore for a couple of days. But I guess we deserved it. Shall we call a truce, now?'

"And we did, of course. Next time he and I made a trip together to the rock, Tark took along a mallet and chisel and carved our two names on the stone. *'Tarquin et Pindar.'* "

"*I* think you should have put *'et Barney'* on it, too," said Mrs. Cheever.

"Well, it didn't occur to us," admitted Mr. Payton, and again the long-ago look of boyhood crossed his face. "But all three of us remained excellent friends. Still are," he added, brightening. "Correspond from time to time. Tark lives in Singapore. Importer. Retired. And Barney lives in Boston. A judge. Still judging."

He went to the screen door, opened it, and leaned out, knocking his pipe against the railing of the stoop.

More than half of the mighty cake was gone. The teapot was cold as a stone. Portia carried plates and cups to the iron sink.

"Do you know what I would like to offer you, children?" said Mrs. Cheever, tying another apron over the one she was already wearing. "Pin, do you know what I would like to offer them?" She paused dramatically. "A house!" she said. "Here are all these old houses! Nothing ever uses them but bats and birds, and some of them are still quite safe. You could pick a safe one and have it for a clubhouse; bring your friends if you wanted. Oh, Pin, wouldn't it be nice to hear children's voices here at Tarrigo again? Though perhaps they wouldn't care for the idea—" she added hesitantly, looking at them.

But Portia, clasping a dish towel to her wishbone cried: "Heavenly! Oh, Mrs. Cheever, what a *heavenly* idea!"

And Julian said: "Brother! Would that be neat!"

7

BELLEMERE

Clouds had covered the sky during the course of Mr. Payton's story, and now as they came out, they saw that the color of the day had changed from green and yellow to a cool gray; the reeds tipping their tops had a velvety bluish look.

"Won't rain yet," Mr. Payton said, glancing at the sky. "Will tonight, though. Eleven, twelve o'clock, we'll get a good, steady soaking. Good for the garden. Good for the frogs."

"My brother has a remarkable talent for foretelling weather," Mrs. Cheever said. "I've hardly ever known him wrong."

"The swamp taught me," Mr. Payton conceded. "Live alone as we do, not bothered by the characters of *people*, and soon, if you're attentive, you begin to know the character of the weather. Or characters. It has many."

They walked the path in single file.

"Now that house," Mr. Payton pointed his cane. "That house, the Delaneys', might be a good one, but there's a bull snake makes his home under the front steps, and I believe there are rats in the basement—"

"No, thank you!" said Portia.

"The Castle Castle has fallen to trash, of course, and the one beyond is unsound. Roof's gone. Same with the Big House. But the Tuckertowns', now. That one, maybe?"

"Let's go see!"

The grass in the dooryard of Bellemere was high as their waists. The old house loomed above them, shabby and fancy. (It doesn't look friendly, thought Portia.)

The front door, glued by years of damp and disuse, stuck fast in its frame. They got in by way of a window, from which the lower sash was gone. The room they entered was large and dark: the floor was littered with fallen plaster, and a crop of toadstools glimmered there.

Portia gave a loud scream, pointing at the wall before them. But then she saw that what she had believed to be a group of approaching strangers, ghosts perhaps, was really only the reflection of themselves. A great mirror was set against the wall.

"I thought it was *people*, not just us," she explained apologetically. "I mean they—we—looked so shadowy and queer—"

"I was startled myself," confessed Mrs. Cheever, "and I knew that mirror was there. It's Mrs. Ravenel's old mirror. She was the mother-in-law. She contributed it to the furnishing of Bellemere. The damp has damaged it now, of course; see how blotched it is? And the frame's turned black. . . ."

Looking into the mirror was like looking into a pond mottled with duckweed. Portia liked the way her face appeared in it: softened, dimmed; mysterious, she thought.

"Now up there on the ceiling where you see the broken fixtures was a very fine gas chandelier," said Mr. Payton, waving his cane aloft. "Wonder what happened to that?"

"Plunderers, no doubt," said his sister. "Plunderers got a lot out of Tarrigo in their day."

Growing used to the dim light, the children's eyes saw now that where the paper had fallen from the walls, names and dates were scribbled and scratched; and initials were carved in the smooth mahogany of the stair rail.

"That's what they *used* to do," said Mrs. Cheever with

satisfaction. "They don't come here any more now that my brother and I have settled in. Perhaps they fancy I'm a witch." She straightened her bell-shaped hat rather proudly.

"It flatters Minnie that folks should think her dangerous," said Mr. Payton, laughing comfortably. "She's about as dangerous as a dove. Now these stairs, Portia, Julian, watch out for *these*. If you select this house, I advise you to mend the treads, Julian; I'll give you the tools. Hold onto the railing, Minnie."

"I'm perfectly able, Pin," replied his sister without holding onto anything but her skirt, to avoid tripping on it. "And I wish you wouldn't call me Minnie! Min is tolerable, but *Minnie!* That's the trouble with the name Minnehaha."

"I know exactly how you feel," agreed Portia warmly. "Everybody calls me Porsh!"

"Well, I never shall. No, indeed I shall not!" declared Mrs. Cheever.

In the upstairs hall Mr. Payton, advising caution, walked ahead, every now and then stamping his booted foot on the floor. "Sound. Seems perfectly sound," he observed. "Roof's still intact, but it's best to be careful; haven't been up here since Nineteen-hundred-and-forty-two."

The rooms that opened off the hall were bleak and empty; clay wasps' nests were stuck to the mouldings. No furniture remained but a broken washstand or two and an iron bedstead. Plaster had fallen everywhere. There was a solid smell of damp.

"That was Tark's room," Mr. Payton observed, glancing at a doorway. "By Jove, how well I remember it. Maps all over the wall. And on his ceiling he'd painted the constellations in their summer order. You can still see some of the blue and gold. He had a time painting it: lay on his back on a plank laid across two ladders. 'That's how Michelangelo painted the Sistine Chapel,' says he. But the amount of paint he got on himself! In his hair! In his eyebrows! 'And I've swallowed plenty, too,' says he, 'for I work with my mouth open when I'm concentrating.' Lucky thing it didn't poison him, though no doubt he had an azure-colored alimentary tract for a long time afterwards."

"I remember those blue eyebrows," said Mrs. Cheever as they continued along the hall. "A terrible sight. Now this room at the very end was Baby-Belle's." She tried to open the door. "Oh, dear, the miserable thing is stuck—Pin, see if you—"

Mr. Payton and Julian shoved their shoulders against the door, which instantly burst open, hurling them inward. Mrs. Cheever and Portia followed.

"This one's lovely!" exclaimed Portia, and it was; a light, spacious room with three windows and a fireplace. Facing south and having been shut up for a long time, the room was dryer than the others, and no wasps had lodged there, though there were signs on the hearth that swifts had nested in the chimney.

Without thinking, Portia walked to a closed closet door and turned the knob. That door, like the other, opened unwillingly, resisting strongly at first and then flying forward to bang her on the forehead.

"Ouch!" said Portia, and then: "Why, look what's up there on the shelf, Mrs. Cheever! Why, look at those!"

Mrs. Cheever put on her glasses in order to peer over them. "Well, I declare! Baby-Belle's old dolls. Well, I vow!" She reached up and plucked one of the dolls from the shelf: a gone-to-seed-looking creature with a chewed-off wig. It had once had eyes that would close, but now its wax lids, like the Bellemere doors, were stuck in their sockets: the eyes met the world with an uncompromising blue-glass stare.

"Corinthia," said Mrs. Cheever musingly, looking at the doll's yellowed petticoats, the little chipped leather slippers. "This is Corinthia Calpurnia (Calpurnia was for Baby-Belle) Tuckertown. I named her myself, and I haven't thought of her in fifty years! Do you suppose the mind ever lets go of a single thing?"

"Mine lets go of arithmetic," said Portia. "And the boundaries of states and things like that. What about these others, though, Mrs. Cheever? What about this fancy one with the turban?"

"Lavinia Lucasta," replied Mrs. Cheever promptly. "I named her, too."

"Even the Tarrigo *dolls* had heavily embroidered names," observed Mr. Payton.

"But why didn't Baby-Belle name them herself?" Portia wanted to know. "One of the things I liked best about them was the naming of them. Long ago when I played with them," she added, glancing at Julian.

"Oh, I was godmother to all the poor things. *This* one, now, came from France, so I named her Nicolette; Nicolette Michelle, in fact. Good gracious, how surprising to remember what you didn't know you knew! She was a present from Mrs. Brace-Gideon on Baby-Belle's tenth birthday. When Baby-Belle opened the box, she said: 'Oh, pshaw! another doll!' (Mrs. Brace-Gideon was not present, thank fortune!) 'Oh, pshaw!' Baby-Belle said, 'I'd rather have a live guinea pig! I'd rather have a B-B gun, or some chewing tobacco!' (Of course she didn't mean *that!*) Oh, she loathed dolls, positively despised them. That's why they were all stuffed away in the closet like that. I used to play with them for her, take them to visit my dolls, so they wouldn't feel neglected."

Overhead in the attic there was now a sound of footsteps and faint voices. Dolls had a limited interest for Mr. Payton and Julian.

"Poor Mrs. Tuckertown, when I think—" continued Mrs. Cheever. "She was such a small, lacy, sweet-perfumed lady. And here was Baby-Belle, taller than her mama by the time she was ten and wearing a two-sizes-bigger shoe! Oh,

87

she must have been a trial to Mrs. Tuckertown! I mean she *loved* her and all, but Baby-Belle was so *big!* And she was such a tomboy. Her hair ribbon never stayed in a bow: it hung down in two long tails beside her face. Perpetually. And she was always up in a tree or climbing a roof or riding a pony bareback. Of course, I liked all those things, too, but I didn't seem to get torn and bruised and dirty quite so devotedly as Baby-Belle did."

She was interrupted by the thunderous descent of Julian from the attic. Mr. Payton followed at a more temperate pace.

"Porsh, listen! The attic's *neat!*" cried Julian. "Just right for headquarters. There's a lot of chairs and trunks and a swell view. A lot of swell views! Come and see."

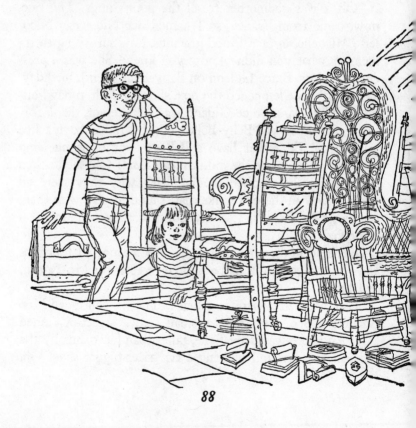

Portia followed him up the steep open stair. Her eyes, level with the floor at first, beheld a grove of chair legs, the sides of painted china hand-basins, a row of flatirons. Coming up into the attic, she saw the humpbacked trunks, the stout chimney like a tree of bricks, the sloped ceilings set with dormer windows. From these, as Julian had said, there were fine views. Facing west, one saw the breathing marsh and the dark vessel of Craneycrow with woods beyond it. To the east lay the broken Bellemere stables and greenhouse, then more woods; and to the south there was part of the shaggy clutter of wrecked houses and the spectacle of Mrs. Cheever's chickens. But at the north there was no window at all, only the brown wooden wall, marked at various levels with names and dates written in white chalk.

"The Tuckertown children's growing-marks," explained Mrs. Cheever, examining them. "Look how little Baby-Belle was way down here in 1887, and then how tall in 1900! A regular Gibson girl she turned into when she grew up—to everyone's astonishment! And then she married a count and went to live in Italy."

"Look here, Min," said her brother, briskly breaking her reverie. "These poor children have a wealth of chairs and washbasins, but what about a table? Does the Big House still afford a table or two? Or are they all congested in your parlor?"

"Indeed they are not! Certainly they may have as many tables as there are. Curtains, too. Rugs. The rugs have provided a balanced diet for generations of moths; but the colors are still pretty—"

"Oh, I adore fixing things up," cried Portia enthusiastically. "And you know something else? I'm glad that the downstairs part is so gloomy and scary, because it makes up here seem even better. It makes a good comparer."

"Let's do have it a clubhouse, Porsh," said Julian. "We'll fix it all up, and then we'll invite some members. Joe Felder, maybe; Tom Parks; guys like that."

"And maybe I can find a girl. There must be some, somewhere. What shall we call it? The Bellemere Club?"

"Na-a. That sounds too much like golf links and a lot of grownups yacketting," scoffed Julian. "I know, though. Why not call it the Philosopher's Club? Even if we're not philosophers and probably never will be."

"Yes. Good. Let's call it that, Jule."

When they turned to Mr. Payton, they were surprised that he should look so pleased.

THE CLUB

Mr. Payton's weather prophecy proved correct. Portia woke for a minute sometime deep in the night and heard the rush of rain. Nice, she thought, turning over; rain is wonderful to sleep to.

It was still raining when she woke for good, and then she was not so pleased. How will we ever get to Gone-Away, she wondered. But get to it they would, somehow; she was sure of that.

Dressing, she looked out of the window at the patient mother dove and wished that she could put a little rain-cape on her. And when she went downstairs, the first thing she saw was Thistle waiting outside the screen door, looking furious. The rain was spoiling all his plans, though the night had been spent profitably catching mice inside the barn.

"Well, don't blame *me*," said Portia, opening the door for him. "I don't like it either."

The day was so dark that Aunt Hilda had the lights on in the kitchen. Foster looked up. "Cinnamon buns," he said laconically, with his mouth full. Perhaps the morning was not ruined after all.

David Gayson had already arrived, of course, and was helping to eat up the breakfast. Uncle Jake, deep in his morning silence, was drinking coffee, and Julian, who had finished, could be heard upstairs battling order into his room.

"Come on, Foss, hurry up, get going, blast off! *I'm*

through," shouted Davey. "Let's go up to your room and build something. I brought my hammer!" Foster leaped to his feet, and they went clattering up the stairs.

"Stair carpet, good and thick. That's the *next* thing," said Aunt Hilda decidedly.

Uncle Jake sighed. "Rain affects small boys like strong coffee, or adrenalin, or snuff. Never saw it fail. Turns them into howling wildernesses. Poor Hilda."

"Oh, I'll survive," she said and gave him a kiss good-by. "I'll put cotton in my ears. I'll run the vacuum."

The noise *was* terrific, Portia thought as she made Foster's bed. (He insisted on sleeping on the top deck, which was the worst one to make.) Aunt Hilda had the vacuum cleaner going full blast downstairs; Foster and Davey were hammering and arguing, and Julian had his record player tuned to maximum volume to shut out everybody else's noise. He was playing the Lieutenant Kije Suite.

In the end, the noise drove Portia to the attic, where she settled down among the Jarman luggage with a very good book called *Wuthering Heights*. Thistle came, too, and purred himself to sleep beside her.

As they were doing the lunch dishes, Julian said in a low, important voice: "Listen, we've got to get to Gone-Away this afternoon! We've got to get started working on the club!"

"Oh, I know," agreed Portia earnestly, as if there were not a moment to lose, and an hour later they were plodding along the wet turnpike with cars slashing past them. Slop, slop, went Julian's rubber boots. Slop, slop, went her own. Rain streamed down her face, and she put out her tongue to lick it from her lip. It tasted flat.

Pushing through the hazel thicket was disagreeable; wet twigs reached up their sleeves and down their necks and into their noses; and as they walked along the old wagon road, random winds above would shake down sudden showers from the trees. But after a while Julian stopped short. "Porsh! Listen!"

"I know," she said, for she had heard it, too: the silvery pealing of a choir of frogs. "There must be a million of them in the swamp."

"I like their singing better than the birds'," Julian said, "because they all know the same tune."

The swamp, when they came in sight of it, was stirring in the wet wind like cats' fur. The broken houses were soaked dark with rain.

"It certainly looks gloomy," observed Portia. "I'm glad we know it isn't."

Mr. Payton, it turned out, was not at home, but Uncle Sam and Florence addressed them with their thin, dry voices, sounding bored and disgusted. The chickens pecked dejectedly among dripping dock-leaves.

"Probably he's at Mrs. Cheever's," Julian surmised. "Come on, Porsh."

As they neared her house, the strains of radio music came forth to meet them, along with a whiff of pipe tobacco and another smell, appetizing and delicious.

As these sounds and scents came from the direction of Mrs. Cheever's kitchen, they went around the house to the back door. Of all the creatures they had seen that day, only the duck looked satisfied.

Mr. Payton and his sister were seated at the kitchen table playing cribbage. From the radio came the neglected strains of the "Habanera" from *Carmen*.

"Why, children!" cried Mrs. Cheever, rising from her chair. "I'm so glad you came, after all. My brother and I feared the weather would prevent you. Just step out of your boots right here on the stoop; I'll put them under the bench, and we'll hang your waterproofs on a chair near the stove. Good gracious, what a day!"

"The frogs like it," Julian said, trying to get his raincoat off without spattering. "That's the most frogs I ever heard in my whole life."

"Lovely; a lovely sound!" said Mrs. Cheever. "They sound like that all spring, and then they stop. Rain starts them piping up again. I guess it makes them think of spring."

"You should hear the big fellows, though," remarked her brother. "There are bullfrogs in this swamp the size of puppies. At night you can hear them, deep and gruff: grunt, grunt, grumble. Like old men discussing the stock market."

"Would you care for a little refreshment?" suggested Mrs. Cheever. "Today I have no cake or cookies, but I *have* got wild blackberry preserve and some of Pindar's honey. And I baked bread this morning."

So that explained the healthy and delicious smell they had noticed.

"But I don't think we ought to interrupt your game," Portia objected feebly.

"Oh, *she* doesn't mind!" said Mr. Payton. "She was losing!"

"I always lose at cribbage," Mrs. Cheever said sadly. "I don't know why I keep on. But I have often beaten him at chess!" As she spoke, she was lifting a cloth from the sleek brown loaves of new bread. She had no refrigerator but a "cool room" in the cellar, and it was from this place that she brought butter and a pitcher of goat's milk.

"We only have butter one week out of the month," she explained. "Just the one week after my brother has gone to town in the Machine. We relish it."

When Portia sipped the goat's milk, she felt like Heidi. But Julian thought it had a strange flavor of goat and did not finish his. He finished everything else, however, and then he and Portia sat waiting expectantly.

"Yes! Tables! Furniture for the Philosopher's Club!" exclaimed Mr. Payton, standing up. "That's what our young friends are concerned with, Minnie. Have you the key to the Big House?"

"Well, you know I have!" replied his sister. "You know where perfectly well." And she went to a church-shaped clock that was tocking on the wall, opened its little glass door, and took out a key.

"It's the only house at Gone-Away that's locked," she told the children. "Except for the Villa Caprice, of course. First though, children, some A.P. Decoction. Rain wakes up mosquitoes, too, you know."

"Don't you need some, too?" asked Portia, when they were anointed with the harsh-smelling fluid.

"Oh, we seldom use it now. It's my belief that we've outgrown the mosquitoes; or perhaps years of using it has discouraged them forever."

Soon they were all on their way, Mrs. Cheever wearing a huge plaid cape of heavy wool. "My husband, Mr. Cheever, bought it for me in Edinburgh fifty years ago," she said. She also carried a great green dome-shaped umbrella that "my husband, Mr. Cheever, bought for me in Tuscany the same year." Mr. Payton wore an ulster and his broad hat. He looked immensely dignified. Slop, slop, went the boots of the children. The chickens, observing the odd procession, made querulous rainy-day sounds.

"Self-pity is the hens' besetting sin," remarked Mr. Payton. "Foolish fowl. How they came to achieve anything as perfect as the egg I do not know! I cannot fathom."

They turned aside at the gateposts of the Big House and steered a course among the tall drenched grass and daisies. Many mosquitoes rose up, adding their thin whine to the frogs' pealing. The Big House *was* big; bigger than Bellemere. It had a flight of wooden steps leading up to a porch, which sagged like the brim of a hat. They tiptoed across this carefully, feeling it tremble.

"Not long for this world, this porch isn't," said Mr. Payton cheerfully. He took the key from his sister, unlocked the door, and he and Julian pushed it open. There was a bright, drafty appearance to the hall in front of them: an avalanche of plaster had buried the stairs. "Roof's gone," Mr. Payton said. "*Been* going for years. Soon the whole place will collapse like the Castle Castle."

Not while we're in it, I hope, thought Portia fervently.

"Maybe we don't really need any tables or things," she suggested.

"Oh, it won't cave in today," he promised her. "Take another storm or two to do the job. *Real* storms, I mean. Now this room," he said, ushering them through an open door, "this was the living room. 'Tisn't much now. Most of what was in it is in my sister's parlor."

One thing that was still in it was the large stuffed head of a moose looking down from a plaque on the wall. It was moth-eaten and melancholy, but its glass eyes still had luster, and between the broad palm-leaf-shaped antlers an antique robin's nest was set like a small turban.

"Now I wonder how long that's been there?" said Mrs. Cheever. "I never noticed it before."

Other things still in the room were two tables, one large, one small, a big carved chest, andirons, and some rolls of carpet. Also an enormous oil painting of a lady with a sloping chin, pale, saintly eyes the size of hard-boiled eggs, and hair that hung sleekly over her shoulders like curls of licorice. Between her dimpled hands was a little book, probably a prayer book, and she seemed loftily unaware of what appeared to be a tornado in the immediate background. Her name, engraved on a plaque in the frame, was Beulah.

"I always detested that woman," Mrs. Cheever admitted. "I am glad to say that she was no relation, just another gift from one of Papa's clients. He hung her in the hall above the console. Baby-Belle despised her, too. 'Sanctimonious old thing,' she used to say. 'Look at her, she hasn't enough sense to come in out of the rain!' "

"Well, we don't need *her* in the Philosopher's Club,

that's for sure," said Julian. "But those tables would be great."

"And the rugs, I hope. Now help me, Pin."

The first one they unrolled disclosed a large mouse's nest, untenanted luckily, and lined with chewed-up letters. Portia saw the date, 3 August 1894, on one of the scraps. The rug was all in holes.

"Oh, everything invades these houses," said Mrs. Cheever. "Birds, bats, rats, mice, moths . . ."

"Hornets," added her brother.

"Mosquitoes," added Julian.

"People, like us," added Portia.

"Yes, and there used to be a family of foxes under the Vogelharts' front porch," said Mrs. Cheever.

The second rug was as tattered as the first, but the third

one, bright red, with a pattern of ferns, was relatively undamaged.

"And there are curtains in the chest." Mrs. Cheever tugged open the carved door, lifted and shook out a length of faded chintz. Then another.

"Don't know how my sister happened to leave them there," commented Mr. Payton. "Why, she'd hang curtains on the coal range if she could. She'd hang them on the hen house. She'd drape them on the goats. She's addicted to the use of curtains."

"Oh, Pin, the way you go on. I declare. Now these, Portia, these portieres hung here in the dining room, and there are five pairs, thank fortune; just right for your club, don't you think?"

"Perfect! They're so nice and red," agreed Portia, fingering the heavy old damask. "But aren't they too good?"

"Better that you should have them than the mice. Now let's see. The rug. The tables. These curtains. The chest is too heavy to move. Is there anything else you'd care to have?"

"I'd like to have the moose," said Julian.

"Welcome to him, then, welcome to him," said Mr. Payton. "But I advise a thorough dusting and a dose of mothballs."

It was agreed that the children would wait to move the furniture until they had cleaned out the Bellemere attic. "And that will be an undertaking," Mrs. Cheever warned. "To my knowledge the place has not been cleaned since nineteen hundred and four."

When they went back to her house, they borrowed a mop, broom, dustpan, many rags, and a bar of soap from Mrs. Cheever; also two buckets of water. Mr. Payton helped carry them to Bellemere, but Portia and Julian took over from there.

For a long time they worked industriously, pushing aside the chairs and empty trunks—all of them were empty, unfortunately—and sweeping the wide board floors, raising clouds of ancient dust except where leaks from the roof had made mud puddles. Portia used the mop to clear away equally ancient cobwebs from the rafters; many of them descended on her. They opened the windows to dump out the dust. Who was going to care? And when they finished scrubbing the floor, they dumped the scrub water out, too. It was a fine way to do housekeeping.

"Oh, let's leave the furnishing till tomorrow," groaned Portia at last, sinking into a rocking chair. "I'm so tired I can feel all my bones calling to me."

"I know. I'm bushed myself."

"Are you ever dirty, too. You look the way you're going to look when you need a shave some day."

"Well, you've got a raggy old cobweb hanging off your bangs. You've got another over your ear."

"Ugh! Get them off will you, Jule? I don't know why it is, but I can't like spiders."

They sat for a while in silence, smelling the cleanness of their attic and admiring their work. Julian was the first to heave himself up. "We ought to go. We've got a long wet walk ahead of us."

"The only way I can do it is on my hands and knees," moaned Portia. A gust of rain scattered against the roof, like gravel.

"What-ho, children!" called Mr. Payton's voice suddenly from below. "Do you know it's nearly six o'clock?"

They descended in a decorous, careful way, Portia leaning heavily on the handrail.

"Tired, are you? I don't wonder," said their friend. "It's still pouring, too. Come, I'll run you home in the Machine."

"Oh, that's all right, sir," said Julian, but without conviction.

"Nonsense, come along. Won't take a minute, and the battery needs exercise."

Mrs. Cheever, sheltered under her green dome, was waiting at the gate. The frogs were still jingling in the reeds.

"I wanted to see you see the Machine for the first time," she said.

"The Machine is a borrowed one," said Mr. Payton. "Permanently borrowed. When we came back to Tarrigo years ago, we had no means of transportation; and our funds were limited. I used to have to walk to town. And then on a visit to the Villa Caprice I found that it was possible to gain access to Mrs. Brace-Gideon's garage. Fortunate. Very fortunate. For there under a tarpaulin was her old hibernating Franklin. Very convenient. An oddity, as you will see, but most convenient."

Mr. Payton had led them to a stable behind his house, and now he threw open the door.

"Voilà!" said he, stepping aside.

"Holy cat!" said Julian.

"For heaven's sake!" said Portia.

Mrs. Cheever was laughing into her hand the way a schoolgirl laughs.

The Franklin was immensely lofty, with great staring headlights like the eyes of a giant shrimp. It was the oldest automobile the children had ever seen; but its red finish was glossy and clean, and the brass fittings were highly polished.

"Think you'll mind riding in an antique?" inquired Mr. Payton. "*With* an antique?" he added.

"I can't wait!" Julian assured him. "Come on, Porsh, you can sit in back."

"Thanks," said Portia, climbing up.

There was a high thronelike feeling to the car when she was seated in it: airy and splendid.

"People build cars too low nowadays," she said. "This way you get a *view*."

"Only trouble with the Machine is she has to be cranked to start. Nuisance. No, thanks, Julian, I'll do it. I'm familiar with her foibles."

Mr. Payton turned the stubborn crank a number of times, and the Machine came to life with convulsive shudderings; it almost danced, and was very loud about it, too.

"Mufflers rusted off," shouted Mr. Payton above the din. "Never had it fixed. Kind of like the racket."

"Neat!" shouted Julian. "Porsh, isn't this neat?"

"Neat!" agreed Portia at the top of her lungs.

"Good-by, children, come soon again," called Mrs. Cheever, waving her green umbrella.

The Machine snorted proudly and started forth. Mr. Payton squeezed the bulb of the brass horn, and it gave a loud trumpet-blast.

There was a roof on the Machine but no sides; the rain came lashing in; and though it did not achieve a speed above twenty miles an hour, there was a full-blooded vigor and clamor about its progress that made it more exciting to ride in than the smoothest modern car, the children thought.

Mr. Payton was shouting something.

"Beg your pardon, sir?" bellowed Julian politely.

"I say it will be a pleasure to meet your family," bellowed Mr. Payton in reply.

"Oh," said Julian. He glanced back at Portia. Heck, then the secret will be broken, he was thinking.

Mr. Payton drove along a rutted road that was new to them. It wound through deep woods and emerged after ten minutes at another point on the Creston Turnpike.

As other cars swept by them, Portia and Julian saw the gaping faces of the passengers; saw the children, transfixed, staring back at them from rear windows. "Get a horse!" shouted one boy, driving by.

Mr. Payton was beaming. "I enjoy the fuss," he confessed. "The Machine always causes a fuss."

They enjoyed it, too, and Julian was trying to imagine how his mother's face would look when she witnessed their arrival. But as luck would have it, she was not there when they drove up; in desperation she had taken the little boys to

a movie. No one greeted them but Katy, barking from the basement.

"Well, another time, another time," shouted Mr. Payton above the Machine. He lifted his broad hat gracefully, and the Machine departed with a stately wobble.

"You know something, Jule?" said Portia as they went indoors. "Maybe Mr. Payton wouldn't like it if he knew he was a secret. Maybe we ought to tell—"

"Oh, no, not yet! I think it's sort of like a sign that, when we come home, nobody's here; as if we *ought* to keep him a secret or something—"

"I'm not so sure about that," said Portia doubtfully.

But then they heard the sound of people running through the rain, and Aunt Hilda and the little boys burst in.

"Saints above!" cried Aunt Hilda, stopping short. "Where in the world did you collect such dirt! And what's that *extraordinary smell?*"

"Smell?" said Julian innocently, with a look of surprise. "Smell, did you say?"

"Just some mosquito stuff, Aunt Hilda," explained Portia truthfully but hastily, dashing for the stairs. "Come on, Jule, we'd better wash!" And when they were up in the hall, she whispered to him: "After this we'll have to wash off the A.P. Decoction every single time before we get home. If you insist on keeping Gone-Away a secret, I mean—"

"And I do," said Julian firmly.

The world looked washed the next day. It *was* washed. Every leaf glittered. The peonies had shed their feathers in the storm, but the roses were at their best.

Portia and Julian set out soon after breakfast, taking their lunch with them, and Julian had also helped himself to a pound of butter from the deepfreeze.

"As a present for them," he told Portia.

He had also borrowed a can of floor wax and a bottle of

Windex. Weighted down by the usual equipment as well as these additions and the lunch basket, they trudged up the wooded way, talking and planning. (By this time they were beginning to make their own path in the undergrowth of the wagon road.)

"We really ought to paint the walls," Julian said. "But let's wait till we get some members to help us."

"I'm going to do the windows as soon as I get there so we can put up the curtains."

"You and Mrs. Cheever! Women and curtains!" said Julian, but he said it amiably.

The reeds of the swamp looked washed, too: green and refreshed. They could see Mr. Payton pottering about his beehives. The little goats were capering nearby and the chickens strutting in the sun. The Machine, newly polished, was taking a sun bath outside the stable, glaring brightly with all its brass. Everything they saw before them delighted Portia and Julian.

"I'm glad we got here good and early," Portia said. "But what is Mr. Payton wearing on his head?"

"A bee veil, I think."

"Good morning, good morning," called Mr. Payton as they came near. "I'm attending to my Caucasians."

"Your what?" said Julian, then remembered to add "sir."

"My Caucasian bees. They're the gentle ones. The Italians I keep in the farthest hive. Can't count on them. Latin temperament."

Mr. Payton's head was draped in a cage of netting. His beard gleamed through it frostily, and he looked like a sorcerer. As he lifted out a frame of honey, the Caucasians crawled over his arms and shoulders and strolled around the brim of his hat.

Portia drew back. "Don't they ever sting you?"

"Only an absentminded one now and then. Usually an Italian," replied Mr. Payton, casting a critical glance at the

Italian hive. "Come back later, children, and we'll have a honeycomb to eat with lunch."

"We will, and here's some butter to go with it," said Julian. "I'll leave it in your kitchen."

"For a present," explained Portia.

"Well, by Jupiter, how pleasant! My sister will be delighted, too. Many thanks, many thanks! Are you off to the club, now?"

"We're going to furnish it today."

"Splendid. Call me if you need any help."

Clanking and jouncing, live as larks, they leaped along the weedy path to Bellemere.

Sunshine flooded the attic. Portia threw open a window, which at once fell like the blade of a guillotine. "Wait till I get some prop-uppers," ordered Julian, running down the open stairs. Soon he returned with five sticks of kindling wood, one for each window.

Portia scrubbed the glass panes with vigor and enthusiasm; Julian, on all fours, polished the floor boards with a will. If their parents could have seen them, they would have been astounded. Through the open windows the sweet in-coming smell of the marsh mingled with the strong practical odors of floor wax, soap, and A.P. Decoction. (Mrs. Cheever had thoughtfully provided a bottle for the use of club members.)

When at last the place was clean enough to suit them, they returned to the Big House to get their furniture. It was hard, hot work hauling the stuff up all the stairs, but when they finally had it in place, after a great deal of haggling and arguing, it looked very fine.

"Jule, it's going to be absolutely beautiful," said Portia, in an awed voice.

"It's going to be terrific. Just wait till I get the moose up!"

"Just wait till I get the curtains up!" said Portia.

They prudently took the moose's head out-of-doors to clean it, but first Julian removed the robin's nest, hard as a teacup, and set it in the fork of a tree. "Next year some robin may be glad of a prefabricated nest," he said.

Clouds of dust and dried moth-wings rose up from the moose when they brushed it; also quite a lot of its fur. Much balder, but cleaner and grander—Julian had used some floor wax to glorify its antlers, and Portia had polished its eyeballs with Windex—the moose was finally installed on the north wall of the attic above the Tuckertown growing marks.

"He looks wonderful there," Portia said. "He makes the room so dignified."

"Terrific," agreed Julian, who was partial to this adjective.

And when the red curtains were up and the red rug was down—with tables and chairs strategically placed to cover the worst of the moth holes—the attic had become a lovely room indeed: cheerful, spacious, bright. Portia ran downstairs with a washstand pitcher, filled it at Mrs. Cheever's pump, and picked a large painful bouquet of roses to put into it. Then, carefully mounting the Bellemere stairs, she set the pitcher on one of the two tables in the attic. It was the finishing touch.

"This is just the best room in the world, that's all it is!" she announced to Julian.

They could not get over it. They kept prowling about the attic, stopping first in one place, then another, to admire their property from different vantage points, gloating over it, congratulating themselves.

"Maybe the rocker would look better over there beside the table."

"The rug should be moved a little to the left, I think. It's crooked."

"I don't believe we should scrub away the growing marks, do you?"

"Oh, never! Leave them. They belong!"

"But we ought to have a picture on the wall."

"Not Beulah, though!"

"No, it has to be the right picture."

They talked and discussed, just as two grownups might talk about and discuss their brand-new house. They were entirely engrossed and never even thought about being hungry until Julian's stomach began to make irritable sounds.

"I don't think we'd better eat our lunch up here, do you?"

"No, we don't want it crumby!"

For a moment they leaned on the sill of the south window looking out at noonday. There was Mrs. Cheever's bell-shaped hat dipping and bobbing above the reeds as she worked in her bog garden. It would appear, sail along the tops of the reeds, and disappear again, as though it were leading a life of its own. Mr. Payton, still wearing his bee hat, was feeding his sister's hens. He had tossed the netting back from his face, and it flapped on his shoulders so that he looked rather like a member of the Foreign Legion. Chickens came clucking and trotting as he shook a sieveful of kernels.

Portia sighed. "You know something, Jule?"

"Hm-m?"

"I wish—"

"You wish what?"

"I wish they weren't so—I wish they were younger."

Julian looked startled. "*They* aren't going to die," he said.

"Everyone does, though. When they get old enough."

"They're *not* old enough. Listen, they lead a healthy life!" He sounded very cross. "They're healthy people. Why, they'll live for years and years!"

"Are you positive?"

"Of course I'm positive!"

Portia felt comforted. They leaned there, watching the bell-shaped hat dipping above the reeds and Mr. Payton's bee veil dipping above the chickens.

As though their thoughts had brushed him, Mr. Payton straightened abruptly, turned and looked up at their window.

"What-ho, Philosophers!" he called, waving the sieve at them. "Come on out in the sunshine, come and talk to me! I've had enough of the company of hens!"

Julian and Portia stormed down the stairs with such a clatter that still more plaster showered from the Bellemere ceilings.

9

THE GULPER

July was drawing to a close. Tiger lilies were blooming everywhere, and in the wasted yards at Gone-Away the chicory flowers hung in a blue veil all spangled and shimmering with white and yellow butterflies.

Portia and Julian had gone there nearly every day; the place had never lost its fascination for them. They were so contented with it that they kept putting off the idea of getting other members for their club. "Oh, there's plenty of time," Julian said. "Let's keep it to ourselves a little longer." And Portia agreed with him.

As for their new friends, the more they saw of them, the better they liked them, and now, instead of "Mrs. Cheever" and "Mr. Payton," they called them "Aunt Minnehaha" and "Uncle Pin." ("We will absolutely never call you Aunt Minnie!" Portia assured Mrs. Cheever.) So the weeks went by, happily and busily, and when the children woke each morning, their first thoughts were of Gone-Away. It was hard not to talk of it at home, but they managed to keep silent.

And then one day at lunch Foster looked at Julian steadily over a long drink of milk, set his glass down, and said: "Where do you and Portia go to all the time?"

"Hm-m? What do you mean where do we go?" Julian buttered a roll slowly as if it bored him, but at the same time he gave Portia a kick under the table.

"I see you. Just about every single day I see you two going off. Always in the same direction, too. *That* way. Where do you go to?"

"No place, really, small fry," replied Julian in an airy, unsatisfactory way. (He had his fingers crossed.) 'No place. Just off."

"I don't believe you. You go somewhere, and I want to know where."

"You wouldn't be interested. Why don't you find Davey and hack around with him? Where's he been all day, anyway?"

"He's sick. He ate something."

"Well, go play with the puppies, then. Go out to the workshop and build something. Draw a rocket ship. *Do* something."

"I don't want to do something. I want to go with you."

"I'm not even sure we're *going* any place," said Julian, still with his fingers crossed.

A little later when they had given Foster the slip (and this was always easy to do, since he was so much younger), Portia felt a pang of guilt.

"Do you think maybe we should let him join the club, Jule? I feel sort of sorry to be fooling him."

"He's too young. When you're six, you can't keep secrets very well."

"Foster can. He really can. He never told about the time I fell out of the window that I wasn't supposed to be sitting on the sill of. He never tells Mother what we've got for her Christmas present—"

"But if we let Foster belong, then we'll have to let Davey belong. And you know what that will mean: 'Bam, bam, zowie, pow! Blast off!' Noise every minute."

"You sound like somebody's old grandfather. And it's not so long since you were making all those noises yourself, Jule."

"Never mind. I'm president of this club, after all, and if I say—"

"Oh, you are, are you? Nobody ever told me. What am I then?"

"Well. You can be the secretary."

"No, I cannot! I don't want to be any dumb old secretary!"

"Okay, *okay*, you can be president, too, then. Gosh. We'll be *co*-presidents. Peace at any price," said Julian, with a loud sigh. "*Girls!*" he added, in a tone of manly exasperation.

"Boys are one hundred thousand million times worse!" retorted Portia. "Sometimes I absolutely loathe all boys." As they quarreled their way up the wagon-road, Foster was completely forgotten by them both.

But he had not forgotten them.

It was not so easy to give Foster the slip when he was on the alert; and today he was very much on the alert, and, in fact, had followed them. He was careful to remain a good distance behind them, walking not on the turnpike but beside it, among the weeds and bushes. Now and then (unnecessarily, since they never looked back), he would freeze and stand still as an Indian in the shadows. Then whispering to himself: "Take it easy now, boy. Look out now; they better not see you!", he would steal forward again. The hours that he and Davey had spent eluding invisible planet men had been good practice. Finally, while standing in frozen position under a hickory tree, he saw his sister and his cousin turn aside, apparently disappearing in a great rank of hazel bushes. But he thought he saw something hanging among the leaves at just the point where they had vanished, and when he reached the place, he found that there was a very withered old sock tied to a twig. He waited cautiously until he heard the arguing voices recede and grow faint; then he plunged into the tangle. Having threshed his way through, he found himself in the woods, standing at the beginning of a weedy road. At the center of this road, pressed into the weeds, there was a path, and he knew who had made it.

"They can't fool you, man," he whispered to himself, and started up the slope. He felt clever and triumphant. He could no longer see or hear Portia and Julian, but now that he had the path to follow, he did not need to. He was sure to find them somewhere at the end of it.

Afternoon sunshine laced the branches and bushes. A catbird creaked in a tree above, and somewhere a woodpecker was drilling. Foster had learned to whistle just the week before, and whistled now, not too loudly (and anyway he couldn't do it loudly), taking great satisfaction in the achievement. He felt satisfied in all directions, in fact, though he did not know what his sister and cousin would say to him when they found that he had followed them all this way like a detective.

"Maybe I won't let them see me," he decided prudently. "Maybe I'll just spy on them and see where they go. That's what I guess I'll probably do."

He stopped to pick up a stone that looked as if it had gold in it, stopped to taste some blackberries (too sour), knocked over a toadstool to see its scarlet pleating, cracked open a hazelnut (too green), and paused to examine a varnished black beetle that was horned like a tiny cow. Then, remembering his mission, he began to hurry.

"So *that's* where they go to," he said a few minutes later, standing screened by leaves and looking down at a great rippling carpet of reeds. In the middle of the carpet stood an island towered and turreted with evergreens; very dark it looked in all that supple, swaying silver-green. But strangest of all were the houses standing beyond the island and the swamp like a row of big, battered castles.

Far away, small as grasshoppers, Foster saw Portia and Julian run up the steps of one of the houses and enter it by way of a window. . . . And now another grasshopper, in a long skirt, came out of a house at the extreme right and started sweeping off the porch, while still another, at the extreme left, was crawling about a garden patch. Near these two houses, on the grass, white chickens were sprinkled like grains of salt.

"Now who are those people?" Foster asked aloud. "What is that place?"

He crept down the hillside, taking cover and freezing from time to time, though not a soul looked up to see him. He thought, as he drew near the swamp, that he could hear the voices of Portia and Julian calling to each other in the house they had entered, but he was not sure; stronger than anything else was the long, poured, sifted sound of wind in the reeds. The reeds were very tall, much taller than Foster was, as he saw when he was level with them; but he parted and entered among them resolutely, certain of his direction. He had decided, when he saw the island, to cut across the swamp and explore it.

Warm water squelched in and out of his sneakers as he walked; very comfortable. Blackbirds hung in the air above him, clucking crossly, and a large bird with a beak like a pair of shears rose up noisily, giving a startled croak. Foster was as startled as the bird.

It took him much longer to reach the island than he had planned. "I'm probably a little bit lost," he said to himself in a sensible, reassuring voice. "Not much, though." He wasn't really worried; he enjoyed the swamp, and during his wandering was able to make the acquaintance of a number of turtles, two black snakes, and the largest bullfrog he had ever seen. He was too engrossed to notice the great cloud-ranges that were growing in the sky.

He floundered and squelched, whistling and talking to himself busily, and at last a sweet smell of pine needles told him that he was near the island; and then he saw it, towering above him.

Just as he reached it, the clouds reached the sun, and color dropped out of the world. A threatening mumble started in the sky, and the wind that crept across the reeds had a new sound suddenly, deeper and graver. "Well, I can't just turn around and go back the minute I finally get here!" Foster said reasonably; but he hurried a little just the same, pushing aside the heavy prickling branches. How sweet they smelled! And underfoot the matted needles were thick as a quilt.

Foster knew he was going to find something on that island, but he didn't know what. He was surprised when it turned out to be a house.

There it stood, under the crowding evergreens, a little gray stone house with a red roof. Drifted needles were piled against the door, and the shutters were closed. Foster didn't think that anyone lived there, but he wasn't sure, and all at once he wished very much that he had never come to the island. He wished with all his heart that he had minded his own business and that he was at home this minute playing with the puppies or just walking around the garden eating something. The little house looked dark and severe under the shadowy trees; it looked like the house of a witch. And it was so still there. The wind seemed to be holding its breath; everything in the world seemed to be holding its breath; Foster, too. . . .

CRASH!

Never in his life had he heard such a thunderclap! It was as if the sky had broken in half! Foster's heart was knocking against his ribs—he could even hear it—and the wind, revived by the blast, began to blow again; suddenly the trees were bending steeply, their branches scraping the roof of the house; and on the heels of the wind came an ocean of rain, and on the heels of the rain, and worst of all, came the lightning snipping and slashing like a razor.

Foster dashed to the door and beat against it with his fists. "Please let me in, please let me in!" But as he ex-

pected, there was no answer. He hesitated a moment, not sure what he feared most: to stay outside in the storm or to enter the dark house, but a blaze of lightning made up his mind for him. He turned the rusty handle, pushed with all his strength, the door flew open, and Foster flew in with it.

The house seemed very dark; he hesitated on the threshold until another great shriek of lightning caused him to bang the door shut and lean his back against it, crying. He was terribly frightened. Only in the brief flares of light that came through breaks in the blinds could he see what the place was like, and then not very well. There was a fireplace opposite him, he saw that; and there was another door, closed, to the left of the fireplace. The room was bare; there was not a stick of furniture in it. It was small, with a peaked ceiling and rafters, and it smelled of pine needles and mildew. Rain drummed heavily overhead, and now and then there was a harsh sweeping sound that terrified him until he realized that it was only branches rubbing against the roof. They scraped at the shutters, too, and squeaked on the window glass where they could reach it; and there was a tap-tap-tapping in the fireplace as rain came down the chimney.

But what were *those?* His eyes, growing used to the darkness, saw two things in the cave of the fireplace, and they were looking out at him; they had eyes! What *were* they? In panic Foster jerked the door open again, ready to run, and then the incoming shaft of light showed him that the two things were nothing but a pair of andirons shaped like owls with yellow glass eyes. They stood with their claws in a drift of pine needles, looking out gravely; not dangerous at all, though not exactly friendly. Foster closed the door again, crying absent-mindedly.

After a while, when he saw that nothing was going to pounce on him and that he probably wasn't going to be struck by lightning, he allowed his sobs to die down and turn into hiccups. He wiped his eyes and nose on his sleeve, found that there was a hook on the door, hooked it, and stepped into the room.

The thunder fell like rocks in the sky, and lightning winked at all the chinks, and each time it winked Foster jumped.

"I don't like lightning by myself," he said to the room. "And I don't like thunder or things shaped like owls."

Though he was not as frightened as he had been, he stood perfectly still in the middle of the room listening to the storm, as if by listening very carefully he could rob the thunder of its threat. After a long time (and he never knew quite how long), the storm began to roll clumsily away; not far away, not gone altogether; it kept coming back for just one more grumble and blast. But each time its force was weaker, and Foster felt greatly encouraged and was able to scratch the dozens of mosquito bites he had collected during his walk through the swamp.

Presently, wanting light, he tried to open a window, then another. But all of them stuck fast, so he opened the door. Wet pine-needles blew across the floor, and there was the bright queer smell of lightning in the air.

Now he could see the place better. The walls, once painted blue, were blotted with stains shaped like the continents on old maps. From the owls' deep nest of needles many had drifted into the room, piling up in the corners. Foster looked at the door by the fireplace.

"Shall I go see what's in there?" he said out loud, and then he said: "Of course you'll go see what's in there!" And he clumped across the floor making a lot of noise and looking stern, and pushed open the door, brave as a lion.

This room was lighter than the other, for one shutter had fallen from its hinge, and he saw that the place was, or had been, a kitchen. There was a little coal range, velvety-orange with rust. On top of it stood a kettle of chipped agateware; when Foster lifted the lid and looked in, he saw only a powder of rust and some dead moth millers. He looked into the oven, too, but there was nothing there except some ancient pie-drippings turned to charcoal. By the window stood a square solid table on which there was a saucer holding a candle that had bent double in the heat of many summers. There were moth millers in the saucer, too, and dozens more hung empty in the soiled cobwebs draped across the glass.

On the table, under thick dust, Foster saw that someone had carved some letters. He cleared the dust away with the palm of his hand, wiped his hand on the back of his jeans, and spelled out the letters. T-A-R-Q-U-I-N.

"Is it a name, or a thing, or what?" said Foster; nor did he know how to pronounce it, whatever it was.

There wasn't much more to examine: a rusty old sink and a rusty old pump; and when he worked the pump handle, all that came out was a rusty old squawk.

But he liked this house, these two little rooms. "Just my size," he said. "Just right for me and Davey." Also he was feeling extremely proud and capable. He had discovered an island, discovered a house, outwitted his elderly cousin and sister, and best of all he had come through a thunderstorm without any grownup, or even Portia, to help him.

After he had explored the house thoroughly, he went outdoors and walked all around it. There was a broken shed, a broken outhouse, and nothing in either of them but moss and mushrooms. Needley branches scrubbed and drenched him, and king-size mosquitoes discovered him with joy.

"Yikes! I'm getting out of here!" yelped Foster, batting and slapping. But first he closed the door of the house securely. "Good-by, house, I'll be back soon," he said to it, feeling as though the nice sheltering little place were really his own.

The fear he had undergone during the storm had driven out any fear he might have felt concerning the reactions of

Portia and Julian. Indeed he felt that he would never be afraid of anything again as long as he lived.

"Well, I'll just go and *tell* 'em," he said stoutly. "I'll just walk across that place to those old houses and *tell* 'em what I did."

So he pushed his way through the showering branches, his hair full of needles, until he came to the outskirts of the island. From there he could look across the swamp at the old settlement. The reeds were glittering in the late afternoon sunshine. Very far away and very small, the thunder rocked back and forth in someone else's sky.

As Foster stepped down into the swamp, the red-winged blackbirds began expostulating again. He was soaked to the skin, bitten and scratched, but he didn't care much. The air was cool, the sponges of moss under his feet were nice to walk on, and he had this fine feeling of accomplishment.

As he made his way among the high reeds, he could no longer see the houses, but he thought he could hear the gabble of hens, so he walked toward that. He didn't hear the voices of Portia and Julian any more, though he paused to listen; and there was no way for him to know that they had started home as soon as the rain had stopped.

When the reeds thinned out, he thought that he must be nearing the row of houses, but then he saw that he was faced with a large expanse of open bog and, beyond that, still another wall of reeds.

"I'll get there, though," he said, watching a bright-blue dragonfly that would zip forward, then stop in the air, then zip forward again, as though it were leading him.

It surprised him very much when the bog beneath his feet began to quake. He was slightly alarmed at first, but when he found that it was perfectly safe, he enjoyed it, even jumping on it to feel the springy swaying. This was better than bouncing on his bed, and nobody was there to tell him to stop. He jumped till he was bored with it, then started on again.

The mosquitoes were bad, and he was tired. He knew it was late, too: the swallows were flying in a late way, in little chattering bunches, in the habit they have when the day's work is done. The bog no longer quaked beneath him, but he had come to a very muddy patch, tufted here and there with hummocks of coarse grass. "I guess I'll just jump from one of those things to the next," Foster decided. Tired, but still nimble as a cricket, he leaped lightly from one tuffet to another, stopping each time to wobble and gain his balance before taking off for the next one.

But after a bit he came to a patch that he knew would be unjumpable for anyone except a kangaroo. He stood on a slowly sinking tuffet looking down at the green-speckled mud. Perhaps it wasn't very deep.

"I'll do it fast," said Foster, leaping from the tuffet.

But the mud *was* deep; he hated the way it came up to the tops of his Keds and then oozed into them. Each step he took sounded as if he were pulling a huge cork out of a bottle; and each time it was harder to take a step at all. The mud was getting deeper, too. Should he go back? He looked over his shoulder, considering. But, as he considered, he sank in farther, and pulled one foot out with a great sucking effort; then the other one. The mosquitoes were singing and settling, and he would have to hurry. The next tuffet was almost within reach, and he saw on it a crown of dark-red flowers with leaves like little trumpets.

Just as he had noticed this and taken two steps more, the world let go beneath him. Down he went: legs, then body, slowly sinking into something that had the consistency of very thick chocolate pudding. He just had time to thrust himself forward and grasp the stems of the dark flowers; they were slippery, and he grabbed a handful of the tough grass that fringed the tuffet instead. But the tuffet quivered and tipped; he did not dare pull on it too hard, though all the time the rich, depthless mud seemed to be drawing him down and down.

A monarch butterfly coasted on the air above his head. The swallows chattered and the blackbirds whistled. Not one of those things knew or cared that he was in such trouble. The mosquitoes probably were glad.

He grasped the shaking clump till all the flowers shivered, calling, shouting, as he had so often called and shouted in play.

"Help! Help me! *Help!*"

10

THE BROKEN SECRET

The afternoon for Portia and Julian had not been satisfactory. Having started off with a quarrel, it kept on hatching quarrels. They had one about the picture, for instance.

On their last visit Mrs. Cheever had given them this picture. They had both admired it on her parlor wall, and she had insisted on taking it down and presenting it to them "for the club." It was really a most wonderful picture, the kind in which you can truly lose yourself. It showed a vast misty view of river winding between huge half-glimpsed crags; in the distance, by the river's edge, a tiny Indian campfire burned with the colors of an opal. You could almost smell the river fog and the harsh spice of smoke, almost hear the lonely dripping of the leaves. . . . Portia wanted to remove the moose and hang the picture in its place. Julian would not remove the moose.

"But, Jule, he could go above the windows on the opposite wall."

"He's better where he is. We'll put the picture there."

"We will not. It's too high up."

"We can hang it just below them, then."

"Oh that's too low down. You know it is. It would look *awful!*"

"Well, heck, then hang it on a string from the ceiling, and we can bang our heads on it. Hang it on the floor. Suit yourself."

"That's a nice way to talk about this wonderful thing. You make me tired, Julian Jarman."

In the end they hung it on the west wall between the dormers. It was a little large; the edges lapped over the wall-corners a bit, but it did look beautiful.

Then they quarreled about what they wanted to do next. Julian was suddenly seized with a desire to see if he could find a way to get to Craneycrow and explore it. Portia was afraid of the Gulper.

"And anyway you know they wouldn't want us to. They'd worry."

"We could just sneak off and not say anything; then they wouldn't have to worry. *I* could anyway, if you're so chicken. . . ."

"I am not chicken! I'm just very sensible. What if we did fall into the Gulper?"

"I can go first and test the way."

"You always go first; *that's* nothing new."

"And if I feel it getting soft, I'll stop. And if I fall in, you can pull me out."

"Oh, great! Or you can pull me in, more likely. . . ."

They were still quarreling when the thunder broke with a bang.

"Now look what you've done," said Julian unreasonably.

"I suppose *I* ordered the thunder? I suppose *I* can do things to the weather?"

"No, but if you hadn't wasted all this time arguing, arguing, *arguing,* we might have been there by now."

"And be caught in a thunderstorm on some dumb island or drowning in the Gulper? No thanks."

"Oh, nuts."

The storm hammered and banged and blazed. Portia wanted to draw the curtains across the windows, but Julian said that would be chicken, and ostentatiously went to stand in a dormer-niche looking out at the storm and trying not to wince when the lightning streaked down the sky in a blinding seam.

What we need is another fellow in this club, thought Julian. And Portia, cowering by the chimney, openly chicken, thought: What we need in this club is another girl.

The roof leaked in seven places. After a while, when she dared to, Portia placed all the available hand-basins and pitchers under the most important ones; the others had just to be let leak. Plink, plonk, chimed water against china. Julian, standing at the window, thought that every time the lightning came the swamp looked startled, caught by surprise. So did all the trees.

Neither of them, even the stalwart Julian, cared to leave Bellemere in this storm and run to Mrs. Cheever's cozy kitchen. But both thought of it with longing.

And after the storm was over, they had to mop the floor and empty the basins and try to dry the rug, and then it was time to go home.

First they went to say good-by to Mrs. Cheever, who was busy making jam. She spoke to them kindly but absently. And when they went to Mr. Payton's house, he greeted them from a window of his attic, where he was mopping up puddles. He also spoke to them kindly but absently.

"A better day tomorrow, philosophers."

"I hope so, sir. Good-by."

"Good-by, good-by." Mr. Payton wrung his mop out and vanished from the window.

As they plodded up the wagon road, Portia and Julian felt bruised with quarrels and thunderclaps, and all the twigs that slapped their legs were wet. The walk seemed twice as along as usual.

And things were wrong at home, too. "Where's Foster?" demanded Aunt Hilda, coming across the lawn to meet them.

"Foster? Not with us," said Julian.

"He's been gone as long as you have. Oh, dear, where *can* he be, then?"

"Maybe he went to visit Davey. Davey's not catching, is he?"

"No, I called Mrs. Gayson. He hasn't been there. Julian, you'll have to go and look for him. Look in the woods."

"Heck, I'm tired."

"You'll just have to forget about being tired, then," said Aunt Hilda, sounding sterner than Portia had ever heard her sound before. "You go up the slope behind the house, and I'll go along by the brook. Call him, Julian, call loud so he can hear you—"

"I'll try the road," said Portia. She was beginning to feel worried, too, and her remorse at having given Foster the slip returned to plague her. I really do like him a lot, she thought. Oh, *why* didn't we take him with us?

Mr. Pindar Payton, having mopped up his attic (first speaking courteously to the hornets), next went out to offer words of comfort and some raw carrots to the goats. Then he walked along the path to his sister's house to see how she had fared. She did not care much for storms, he knew, though he enjoyed them himself. However, he found her busy in her kitchen, quite unperturbed, making raspberry jam.

"Thank fortune I picked them all this morning," was her greeting. "Dead ripe. The storm would have ruined them."

"Delaney berries or Vogelhart?"

"Vogelhart. I did Delaney's last week. They always ripen first."

The kitchen smelled delicious, sweet and syrupy. In spite of Mrs. Cheever's industry it was, as usual, in spotless order; and there was something new to decorate it: the oil lamps had been moved into the pantry, and on the bracketed shelf sat all of Baby-Belle Tuckertown's old dolls. "Well, I just hated to think of them shut up in the dark," Mrs.

Cheever had said defensively when her brother voiced surprise. The dolls all had new dresses, too, though distinctly out of date in style; and the ones who had lost their hair wore colored caps and turbans.

Mr. Payton went into a room that they called "the library" and came back with one of his ancient newspapers. He settled himself in his particular chair with his pipe and a glass of cherry-mead, while his sister puttered at the stove. The clock on the wall had an easy-going sound. Now and then Mr. Payton would tell his sister about something he was reading in the paper.

"On July the 29th, nineteen-hundred, at Heathen's Crossing, Massachusetts, a baby boy was born with five teeth."

"I declare," said Mrs. Cheever peacefully. "July 29th. That's today, isn't it?"

"Well, Min, you know I always try to read a paper of the same day. The year doesn't signify."

"No, I suppose not." Mrs. Cheever began pouring the crimson jam into hot jelly-glasses.

"The King of Italy was assassinated on that day, too. I'd forgotten that."

"Well, well. Poor soul," said Mrs. Cheever. "Look, Pin, isn't this a lovely color?"

"Like all the rubies of Golconda," replied her brother. There was silence for a while, then Mr. Payton said: "Now here's an item, Min. Did you know that in nineteen-hundred you could have bought a full-length sealskin coat for—"

"Wait! Pin! Listen!"

"What's up?" Mr. Payton lowered his paper. His sister was standing transfixed, one hand raised for attention.

"Listen!"

"By George, it's a child!"

"*Help, help!*" The words came faintly, but they heard the terror in them.

Mr. Payton threw down the paper and ran for the door. "Wait! Minnie! Where's your clothes pole?"

"By the clothesline, of course. Oh, Pin, is it someone in the Gulper?"

"Don't know. Sounds like it." He was off and she was after him, her long skirts catching on the weeds, but he soon left her far behind.

"Hang on there, whoever you are!" shouted Mr. Payton. "Help's on the way! Hang on!"

"I'll try," called an obedient, frightened voice. "But please hurry up."

Foster thought, when at last he saw Mr. Payton break through the reeds, that Santa Claus, or maybe even God, had come to rescue him in person. He had never seen a real live snow-white beard before.

"Now take it easy, son. I'm going to stand right here, see? I can't come further, but the clothes-pole will reach. You take hold of it; hold *hard*, son, and I'll just pull you, *tow* you in. But don't let go."

"Okay," quavered Foster. "But I'm kind of weak from scaredness."

"No, no, you're not! Grab it tight; that's right. We'll have you out in no time."

And in a minute Foster *was* out, on firm footing again and black as the Tar-Baby.

"Oh, Pin, the poor little mite! Bring him straight home." The lady who had just appeared looked odd even to Foster: such a long queer dress, such strangely shaped sleeves; and on her head a red velvet bow was quivering. "What is your name, child?"

"I'm Fos—I'm Foster Blake," he said. His teeth were chattering. Mr. Payton took off his jacket and wrapped it around him.

"But it'll get all mu—all muddy."

"Pshaw, mud's not important. Take my hand, son; we'll be there soon."

"Foster Blake," repeated Mrs. Cheever, trotting rather breathlessly behind them. "Then you're Portia's little brother, aren't you?"

"Yes, I am. Do you know her?"

"Oh, very well. We're Aunt Minnehaha and Uncle Pin. They've told you all about us, I know."

"N-no, they never have."

"They *haven't?*"

"N-no. I wondered where they went off to every day. They wouldn't tell, so I f-followed them. Th-that's why I'm here n-now."

"I declare," said Mrs. Cheever thoughtfully. "Pin, do you suppose they've kept us secret?"

"Begins to look that way. I wondered why they never brought this one along, the rascals."

"I guess they'll be m-mad at me when they see me now."

"They won't see you yet; they've gone home. And

when they do, they won't be angry, I'll wager," said Mr. Payton. He sounded very sure.

At Mrs. Cheever's house Foster had an interesting bath in a wooden washtub. Mr. Payton explained that though there was a bathtub upstairs, the plumbing had been out of order for fifty-two years. Foster had two baths in succession; one wasn't enough.

"And now just see what we've found for you," Mr. Payton said, tapping on the door. "These were our brother Lex's clothes when he was about your age. There was a trunk full of children's clothes in the Big House; nobody knows why. You can wear these home."

Foster did not care for the clothes at all, but he couldn't possibly wear his own, so he put the strange garments on reluctantly, beginning with a suit of most peculiar underwear, which had long sleeves and legs and buttoned down the front with hard bone buttons. Over this he was persuaded to add a sort of vest with hanging garters and a pair of black-ribbed stockings (Yikes! Stockings!); next came a shirt with a collar that felt like a dish, a large fluffy tie tied in a bow, and a suit with short pants made of some very scratchy stuff that smelled strongly of camphor and black pepper. Foster sneezed.

The finishing touch was a pair of Mrs. Cheever's bedroom slippers: kid, with wilted silk pom-poms. Foster took one look at himself in the mirror and never looked again.

"Did boys really wear things like this, ever?" he said, coming into the kitchen.

"You should have seen what the poor girls had to wear.

Flannel petticoats, for instance," replied Mrs. Cheever.
"Now, dear, do you think you could eat something?"

Foster said he thought he could.

It was a wise decision. He was given fresh homemade
bread and fresh homemade raspberry jam—still warm
and the best he'd ever tasted. Also a large cup of cambric
tea with enough sugar in it for once.

"I like this place," said Foster. "What is this place? Has
it a name?"

So they told him all about Tarrigo turned Gone-Away.
And then he told them all about his expedition to "that
little island in the middle."

"You *got* to it? Tell me, is the house still standing?"

"Yes, that's where I stayed while it thundered."

"It still has a roof?"

"Yes; a roof and a stove and two things shaped like owls
in the fireplace—"

"Oh, *those!*" exclaimed Mrs. Cheever. "My goodness
gracious, I remember those! Mrs. Brace-Gideon gave them
to Mrs. Ravenel, but Mrs. Ravenel couldn't abide them—"

"Mrs. Brace-Gideon had an unusual talent," said Mr.
Payton. "She seemed to know exactly what a person didn't
want; and then she would go out and buy it and give it to
him."

"Well, Baby-Belle, my friend, persuaded Mrs. Ravenel,
her grandmother, to let us have those owls for Craneycrow—"

"That's the name of your island," explained Mr. Payton.

"—and we were delighted. They looked so witchful."

"I didn't like them at first," said Foster. "But then I liked
them."

"And now I think we'd better go," said Mr. Payton.
"Your family must be worrying, Foster, and we have no
telephone."

"We have nothing modern in the whole place except the
radio," said Mrs. Cheever with pride.

"And that had its nineteenth birthday last December," added her brother. "Well, let's be off."

As Foster stood up, Mrs. Cheever clapped a large flat thing on the back of his head: some kind of hat. It was held on by means of a band under the chin, and Foster didn't like it at all, but thought it might be rude to take it off.

Mrs. Cheever was putting on a large queer hat herself, tying it down with a veil.

"Are *you* coming with us, Minnie?" said Mr. Payton in surprise.

"Yes, this time I'm coming, too," replied Mrs. Cheever, "for I refuse to be a secret any longer."

"I've just called Uncle Jake, Portia, and he thinks I'd better phone the police," said Aunt Hilda, coming out to the porch where Portia and Julian, properly subdued, were sitting on the railing. All three looked frightened and discouraged. Nobody, naturally, had seen a trace of Foster. "I'll do it right away," said Aunt Hilda, turning to the door.

And then, just at that instant, all of them were made aware of an extraordinary noise: an approaching noise that grew louder and more violent as it came nearer. Aunt Hilda whirled around and stared.

Never, as long as she lived, did she forget the spectacle she saw. There, jiggling clamorously toward the house, came an equipage that looked more like a gigantic insect than a car, and throned on its high back were three people from another era: an elderly lady wearing a motor-veil and duster, an elderly gentleman with an elegant beard, a little boy with a round hat on the back of his head like a blue-serge halo. And then she saw that the little boy was Foster.

As she ran forward, nearly weeping with relief, several wild conjectures raced through her mind. Could Foster have been lost in another dimension of time? Had he somehow slipped into the past and brought it back with him?

"Hey, Uncle Pin!" shouted Julian.

"Why, Aunt Minnehaha!" shouted Portia.

"How'd you find him?" shouted Julian.

"And *where?*" shouted Portia.

Aunt Hilda with her arms around Foster stared at them both. "Do you *know* these people?" she demanded, too puzzled to be polite.

"Oh, yes, they know us very well," replied the gentleman, stepping down and sweeping off his hat. "But just today we found we had been kept a secret. Allow us to introduce ourselves. I am Pindar Payton, and this is my sister Mrs. Lionel Cheever. You are Mrs. Jarman, I presume?"

"Yes. Julian's mother. How—how do you do? But children, *why? Why* didn't you tell me about your friends?"

"Julian was the one who wanted them kept secret," said Portia cravenly, but then she added: "I agreed to it, though."

"I just thought—well, you know, I just thought it would be nicer that way. I mean, sort of more fun," explained Julian lamely.

"Perhaps it would have been better to consult us," said Mrs. Cheever. "But never mind; no harm's been done."

"And *he* saved my life," said Foster, nodding his head at Mr. Payton. "I was drownding in mud—"

"He *did?* You *were?* Oh, please," cried Aunt Hilda, clutching at good manners again, "please come in and sit down and tell us all about it."

"Well, perhaps for just a moment," said Mrs. Cheever, descending daintily from the Machine.

Julian said to Foster: "You mean you really fell into the Gulper?"

"I don't know it's name, but I fell into it. All mud. I was drownding. I didn't like it."

"That was the Gulper, all right," said Julian. (Boys are

certainly peculiar, Portia thought; he almost sounded jealous.)

In the house Aunt Hilda hastily brewed some tea, and then they all settled down to the business of becoming acquainted. Portia saw Aunt Minnehaha's glances darting about the room appraising the furniture, the colors, the pictures on the wall. It had been so long since she had seen any house but those at Gone-Away.

A great deal of talking and explaining and thanking went on, and in the middle of it Uncle Jake came home, and having just been badly startled by the Machine in the driveway, he gaped at the strangers and his own nephew, all in antique costumes, lost *his* manners, and blurted out: "What's this, a masquerade?"

"Jake, this gentleman, Mr. Payton, saved Foster's life," said Aunt Hilda in a dignified voice.

So then the explaining began all over again, and then more thanking and more tea-drinking, and suddenly Uncle Jake turned to Mr. Payton and said: "Sir, I wonder if you'd care to have a dog?"

"I beg your pardon?" said Mr. Payton.

"We have an abundance of dogs in our basement. Boxer pups. Nothing on earth could begin to express our appreciation to you for saving Foster from becoming a permanent mud-pie, but I just thought—perhaps—a dog . . ."

"Fatly wouldn't like it," said Portia.

"Then Fatly will have to make the best of it," retorted Mr. Payton. "A good dog is just what we've been wanting. Fatly will have to join your club; become a philosopher."

"That's never hard for a cat," said Mrs. Cheever.

Then they all went down to the basement to view the puppies, each one named by now. The female was called Prune, and the four males were Gulliver, Othello, Tarquin, and Tarrigo.

"I wondered where in the world Portia got those two names!" Aunt Hilda said.

"Oh, Tarrigo, don't you think, Pin? We must have Tarrigo!" cried Mrs. Cheever. "Look at his folded little face! See what a bold fellow he is!"

"He seems a splendid animal," agreed Mr. Payton. "Do you think he's old enough to leave his mother?"

Uncle Jake assured him that he was, and when Mr. Payton and his sister re-entered the Machine, they had a third passenger, plump and lively.

When all the farewells had been said and the engine cranked up, Foster ran to the Machine, shouting something.

"What's that?" Mr. Payton shouted back, cupping his ear and leaning out.

"I said thank you very much for saving my life!" called Foster.

"Oh, any time!" called Mr. Payton, putting the car in gear. "Delighted, any time at all!"

They stood watching the Franklin prance away.

"They've got another modern thing besides their radio," Foster remarked. "They've got that license plate."

Aunt Hilda put one arm around Julian's shoulders and the other around Portia's and said: "I think it was extremely selfish of you both to keep those charming people a secret for so long!"

MEMBERS

"Minnehaha," said Mr. Payton the next day, "I have determined to defeat the Gulper."

"But how?" inquired his sister, well aware of the seriousness of his decision by the fact that he had used her full first name.

"I shall defeat it by bridging it!" declared Mr. Payton.

"But how?" repeated Mrs. Cheever.

"That's the problem: a system of pontoons, perhaps. Perhaps a simple plank and piling structure. *Something,* anyway."

"Oh, Pin, you may fall in!"

"Pshaw, of course I won't fall in!"

"But supposing there are other Gulpers? You can't bridge them all."

"If one is bridged, the others won't signify, as far as people are concerned, anyway. They'll be warned always to use the footbridge. And we've got the location of one Gulper well established: I marked it with the clothes pole."

"Well . . . I'll need another clothes pole, though," said Mrs. Cheever, running out of objections.

When Julian arrived that afternoon, he was alone. "Portia's busy making friends with a girl," he said, sounding rather forlorn (though he certainly didn't intend to). "She's Davey Gayson's cousin, Lucy something-or-other, and they've been yakking away and yakking away all morning like a couple of squirrels. I just thought I'd come over by myself and do some collecting or something. . . ."

"No, sir, Julian, I'm going to put you to work," announced Mr. Payton. "I have an engineering problem ahead of me, and I think you may be able to help me solve it."

As soon as he heard what the project was, and that it involved a certain amount of risk and a lot of mud, Julian brightened visibly.

"Then I'll get to see Craneycrow myself!"

Building materials presented no problem. "Gone-Away is nothing if not a lumberyard," said Mr. Payton. "We ought to be able to locate good pilings at the Castle Castle. If not, we'll try the old Humboldt place."

Wild cucumber vines, frosted now with green-white flowers, mantled the vast heap of rubble that had been the Castle Castle. Burdocks grew there, too, and thistles and woodbine; the ruin was apparently very nutritious for weeds. They had to rip their way in. Julian got a splinter in his thumb, and Mr. Payton barked his shin on a concealed brick pier. The innumerable inhabitants of the lumber heap were sent scuttling and scooting: beetles, sow bugs, ear wigs, moths, spiders, ants, centipedes, and one tall tiptoeing daddy-longlegs. Julian and Mr. Payton rooted happily in the rubbish of the fallen house, and at the end of an hour had unearthed eight strong oak posts suitable for pilings. "The Castle's porch posts," said Mr. Payton. "See, here's one of the hammock rings still fastened to one. By Jupiter, I remember the sound of that hammock! It croaked like a pheasant all through the summer evenings."

By the time they had collected a number of planks and several yards of fancy railing, Julian had also been bitten by a click beetle ("and they're not supposed to bite!" he said in outrage) and Mr. Payton had torn his jacket sleeve on a nail. Both had picked up a liberal supply of stick-tight burs, and Mr. Payton even had a few applied to his beard.

Damaged and extremely dirty, but feeling well satisfied, they hauled their findings to the edge of the path and laid them down.

"Tomorrow I'll bring my barrow and we'll get to work," said Mr. Payton. "But that's enough for now. Julian, there's a certain watermelon in my patch, and I can hear it calling me by name. Come!"

After they had washed some of the dirt off at the pump, Mr. Payton lifted down his conch shell, blew into it, waited for the other shell's reply, and then placed three chairs on the grass before his door.

Soon they saw Mrs. Cheever come tripping along the path. She was wearing a lavender-patterned dress trimmed with lace and had pinned a bunch of pansies to her hat.

"I *thought* I was being summoned to a watermelon, so I took precautions," she said, and shook out a raincoat, which she put on. "I'm very partial to melon, but I don't like to worry when I'm eating it. No, indeed I do not!"

The watermelon, cut open, was red as a sunrise and cold as snow. Nobody said anything for a while. There was a juicy sound of watermelon-eating and the contented buzzing of hornets going in and out of the upper windows. Tarrigo, tied to a long tether, sharpened his teeth on a bone while Fatly watched him critically from the gatepost.

"Fatly doesn't seem to mind him much, does he?" said Julian.

"Fatly can afford to condescend. Tarrigo seems very young and crude to him still," explained Mr. Payton. "Here, more watermelon, son . . ."

After another juicy silence, Julian said: "You know what I think, Uncle Pin? *I* think it's time we got a few more members: guys to help us with the bridge and things like that. What do you think?"

"An excellent idea," agreed Mr. Payton, dabbing watermelon juice from his beard with a frayed silk handkerchief. "I confess I feel a little tired."

Mrs. Cheever was gathering up rinds with which to give the goats a treat. "I also have a suggestion to make," said she. "*I* think it would be nice if Foster were allowed to join. Indeed I do. After his experience with the Gulper and all, poor mite!"

"Oh, Porsh and I've decided that already!" Julian assured her. "We decided it this morning before breakfast."

Portia liked her new friend Lucy Lapham very much: they had a great deal in common. Both wore tooth braces, weighed eighty-five pounds, and were the same height; both had had measles (the same year!) but not mumps; both liked studying English but hated arithmetic, preferred the color green to all other colors, wore size three shoes, and had birthdays within a week of each other in October. "And that means," said Lucy, "that we have the same sign of the zodiac—"

"Libra!" said Portia.

"And the same birthstone—"

"Opal!" said Portia.

However, there were differences. Lucy was passionately interested in baseball, for instance, and Portia was ignorant about it. Lucy favored the Giants, and Portia the Dodgers (only because Julian did). Portia had straight tan hair, and Lucy's was dark and curly. But these differences were not important.

"Let's be best friends while I'm here, okay?" suggested Lucy.

"Julian's my best friend," said Portia loyally. "But you can be my second-best."

"I'll be your best *girl* friend," decided Lucy. That sounded better.

They wandered to and fro, talking: across the lawn with their arms around each other's necks; up into a large maple tree as high as they could go and down again; into the brook for a cooling wade and back across the lawn, still talking every minute.

"Boys are all right," Portia said. "At least my cousin Julian is; he's *very nice*. But if you really want to talk, give me a girl!"

"That's just exactly what *I* think," said Lucy.

"Promise never to call me Porsh, though."

"Okay, if you'll promise not to call me Lu."

"I swear I never will."

They took turns on Foster's swing, still talking. "There's something I'm just dying to tell you about, Lucy," said Portia, flashing back and forth against the summer sky. "But I have to get Jule's permission: it's half his secret."

"What is it? Oh, tell me, Portia, *come* on!"

"No, I honestly can't, now, but maybe tomorrow I can!"

"Heck," said Lucy.

But things worked out very well. When Julian came home, covered with stick-tights and wood powder and reeking of A.P. Decoction, he said: "Hey, Porsh, is it all right with you if I elect a couple of guys to the club? We need workers."

"It's all right with me if *I* can elect a girl," she replied. "I've got one all picked out."

The next two days it rained without stopping, and though they did not go to Gone-Away, Portia and Julian were not idle. They selected their members and elected them at the same time: Joe Felder and Tom Parks for Julian; Lucy Lapham, of course, for Portia. Only after they had elected them did they trouble to seek out the members of their choice and inform them of the honor that had been conferred on them. And then they had to explain about the club.

"What's the purpose of this club?" Joe Felder asked, and Julian said: "Well, I don't know if it's exactly got a purpose, has it, Porsh?"

"Fun!" said Portia.

And they told them about the curious location of the club, and about its sponsors, Mr. Payton and Mrs. Cheever.

"That old man!" exclaimed Tom Parks. "Why I've seen *that* old man in his crazy old car! Everybody in Pork Ferry laughs about him. They say he's nutty as a fruitcake. . . ."

"They say he's got a sister even nuttier that never goes anywhere," contributed Joe. "They say that's *why* she never goes anywhere."

"Listen!" ordered Julian. "You wait! These people are— why, they're *terrific!* They're great! The greatest! *Aren't* they, Porsh?"

"They're the best, nicest, most wonderful grownups I ever knew, next to my father and mother and uncle and aunt and my English teacher at school!" Portia declared hotly.

"Listen! You guys talk like that around here and we'll un-elect you, that's all! We didn't *have* to elect you, you know!"

"Oh, take it easy, Jule," Tom Parks said. "If you say they're okay, *okay*. We never even met them."

"*I'm* not talking like that," Lucy pointed out virtuously. "*I* think they sound lovely."

"And anyway we'd like to be in your club and see that

place and all," said Joe Felder. "I've heard about Gone-Away, but I never did see it."

"Well, tomorrow, if the rain ever gets through raining," said Julian, glaring darkly at the window, "we'll go and spend the day. Everybody'll have to bring his own lunch, though. And another thing: this is a secret club. I mean you can tell your parents if you absolutely have to, but no one else, see!"

They promised. All of them believed a secret club to be the best kind.

The next day, luckily, was perfect: a blue and yellow summer day. According to plan, the children met on the turnpike, at the "Sign of Ye Old Red Sock," as Julian had put it. They scrambled through the hazel bushes, which were still wet, and up the grassy wagon track, which was also still wet, but who cared about that?

"It's a pretty long walk, isn't it?" remarked Tom Parks after a while. He was rather fat and carried the largest lunch basket.

"Worth it, though," Portia assured him.

"Gee, I always did want to see Gone-Away," Joe Felder said. He was a tall boy with curly brown hair; he was going to be very handsome, but he didn't know it yet. Neither did anybody else.

At last they reached the top of the ridge, crossed it, and came to the clearing where the first view of Gone-Away could be seen.

"There!" said Julian with quiet pride, as though he himself had manufactured the scene before them.

"Man!" said Joe Felder, stunned.

"Nobody ever told me about this place in my whole life!" Tom Parks sounded indignant. "Here's this neat place right near home, and no one ever even told me!"

"I think it looks a little scary, though," quavered Lucy. "Doesn't it? Don't you think it does, Portia?"

"I did just at first. But it isn't, honestly. It's the best place there ever was; it's got everything!"

"There's Mr. Payton milking Florence," said Julian. "Come on, you kids, you have to get introduced."

The morning passed like a dream. There was so much, and all of it so interesting, to show the club members. They were introduced not only to Mr. Payton but to Mrs. Cheever, to Tarrigo, Fatly, the goats, the duck (the chickens didn't count; they never do), the bog garden, the houses, and last of all the club.

"Hey, this is terrific!" cried Tom Parks, staring at the wonderful room.

"You mean it's really ours to keep? And all the things in it? To use *forever?*" said Joe Felder unbelievingly.

"That's what *they* say."

"Man! That picture, even?"

"Everything."

"And *they're* so nice," said Lucy. "No wonder you're crazy about them."

"Next time I see him being laughed at in Pork Ferry, I'll have something to say!" promised Tom.

"Me, too," said Joe.

After lunch (which they ate in the shade of a willow tree at the Vogelhart place), the boys and Mr. Payton set off to start construction on the bridge. Portia and Lucy engaged in a little light housekeeping. Very light. They kept stopping to talk, Portia leaning heavily on her broom, and Lucy standing with a dustpan in one hand and a dust brush in the other.

Mrs. Cheever brought a chair out to her front porch and sat there mending. Now and then she would put her work down, close her eyes, and lean her head back, smiling. Young voices coming from the swamp; young voices coming from the Tuckertowns' old house! When she closed her eyes like that, she could almost believe that this was Tarrigo again and she herself was still a child.

12

THE SUMMER CATS

August was a perfect month that year. Perhaps the farmers didn't think so, but the children did. Nearly every day was sunny, and nearly every day all or several of the members of the Philosopher's Club were to be found at Gone-Away. Foster and Davey came, too, when they felt like it, and sometimes even a few grownups made the journey. One of the things that made August wonderful for Portia and Foster was the fact that their father and mother had come to spend the month, and of course they were told about the club almost before they had stepped from the train.

"There's this place where I almost drownded in the mud where we have a club!" shouted Foster, leaping at his mother and hugging her hat off.

"A club in the *mud?*" said his mother.

"No, near it, beyond it by the swamp. By *Gone-Away*. You know. I wrote you about it," Portia explained.

"Oh, there. Good. I can't wait to see it."

It was lucky, Portia often thought later, that everybody, even grownups, seemed to like Aunt Minnehaha and Uncle Pin; and equally lucky that Aunt Minnehaha and Uncle Pin always seemed to like the right grownups.

Quite often now, when they went to Gone-Away, Portia's mother and Aunt Hilda would amble slowly up the wagon road behind them, talking together, the way grown-up ladies always seem to amble and talk. When I get big, I'm going to still *run*, Portia said to herself. I'm going to still jump if I feel like it, or hop on one foot.

Mrs. Cheever was always pleased and excited when the grownups came. Her velvet bow would begin to quiver like a butterfly, and her first thought was of offering them "a little refreshment." When they left, they were often the richer by a jar of jelly or pickles; by a present of dried summer-savory or pennyroyal, or a small china ornament "from the Big House," and always by a lingering odor of A.P. Decoction, since mosquitoes are no respecters of persons.

"Now I understand what that smell *was*," Aunt Hilda said.

But when she or Portia's mother begged Mrs. Cheever to return their visits, the old lady always refused.

"No, my dear," she said steadfastly. "I am a true snail. I do not like to leave my own shell, and I mean never to leave it again. But whenever *you* wish to come to *me*, I shall be overjoyed."

And so they often came.

The bridge was progressing nicely. One end of each porch post had been whittled to a point like a giant pencil, and each pencil was then driven into the swampy mud with a mallet that Mr. Payton had made of a straight hickory limb and a block of hard maple. The double sound of blow and echo resounded every day among the reeds, and the blackbirds were outraged. The boys enjoyed the work, but Portia and Lucy after two days of helping decided to help no more.

"I've had enough mud to last me the rest of my days," said Lucy.

"It's more boys' kind of work, anyway," said Portia, dismissing the whole project.

They preferred to visit with Aunt Minnehaha, or wander in the woods, or explore the dilapidated houses, or pick the blackberries, which were ripe now and glossy as jet. There was an ancient sleigh behind the Humboldt house, lashed to the earth with bindweed; sometimes they sat there and talked. Sometimes they went to the bog and collected mosses for Japanese gardens. There was never any lack of things to do.

One afternoon Mrs. Cheever took them to an upstairs room in her house and presented them with a trunk full of ball gowns to dress up in.

"But you might need them sometime," said Portia, looking covetously at the array before her.

"*Ball* gowns? Hardly!" said Mrs. Cheever, laughing.

The dresses had belonged to her and her sisters long ago, and there were others of still an earlier date that had been their mother's.

"You were a very keeping family, weren't you?" said Portia, lifting out a heavy satin dress yellowed with age.

"Yes, we were, thank fortune. I'll never run out of clothes as long as I live. Now that dress, Portia, the one you're holding, was made by Worth, a famous dressmaker in Paris. My sister Polly had that one. I was allowed to come down in my nightgown just to look at her the first time she wore it, and, oh, she was a vision! Her husband proposed to her that very night after a ball at the Jaspers' in Attica! See, dear, let go of the dress; see how it stands there by itself! They knew how to spin a satin in those days!"

Dress after dress was lifted from the trunk: silk and satin and velvet and taffeta, and a material called mull. Time had frayed and faded some of them, but many were still perfect. All had a dry smell of age and camphor, and from a few came the faint ghost of perfume.

Portia struggled into the Worth ball gown, losing her way several times.

"My heavens, Aunt Minnehaha, how old was your sister when she wore this? How *big* was she? I can't make it meet around my stomach!"

"Why, I believe she was nineteen, but in those days young ladies took great pride in their small waists. Polly's was twenty inches around, which she considered rather stout. Helena Humboldt's, now, was only seventeen inches when she was laced!"

"Laced?"

"Corsets. Let me see. Here's one."

"My heavens," said Portia.

Lucy tried the corset on over her shirt and blue-jeans. It made her look like a peculiar sort of gladiator. When Mrs. Cheever drew up the laces at the back, Lucy gasped.

"Ow! My ribs are crunching; I can't breathe!"

Mrs. Cheever released the laces, and Lucy burst forth with a loud sigh of freedom.

"I'm glad I live in wide-waisted days!"

"And in blue-jean days," agreed Mrs. Cheever. "Oh, how Baby-Belle would have envied you! I remember the time we rescued the summer cats—"

"Summer cats?" said Portia and Lucy together.

"Mrs. Brace-Gideon's summer cats. When you girls have made your selection, we'll go down and have some lemonade and I'll tell you about it."

Portia decided to wear the Worth gown anyway, unfastened at the waist. Mrs. Cheever covered the unseemly gap with a broad striped sash. "Roman," she said, tying a large bow at the back. "My Aunt Eulalia brought it to me when I was seven, and I wore that sash to every birthday party I ever gave or went to till I was sixteen years old!"

Lucy selected a dress that had belonged to Mrs. Cheever's mother. A collapsible bone crinoline went with it.

Mrs. Cheever clicked her tongue. "I often wonder what the good Lord thinks of the way we put his creations to use! Just imagine, it took a whale to supply these parrot-cage petticoats for ladies. A great whale of the deep!"

The dress that went over the parrot cage was made of a bold blue silk, trimmed with velvet ribbon and scores of little buttons that didn't button anything.

"Well, I can't make this one meet around *my* middle, either," said Lucy.

"Never mind, here's another sash. This one was Persy's. There, now, you both look beautiful; look in the mirror."

"My wishbone sticks out too much," said Portia severely. "My elbows are too pointy."

"Time will cushion them," Mrs. Cheever told her comfortably.

But Lucy said nothing about herself because she thought that she looked perfectly beautiful; the dress was very becoming. As they went downstairs, the great skirt billowed and swayed about her legs. "I feel like a schooner with wind in my sails," Lucy said.

"You look more like a blimp," said Portia.

They took the cool pitcher out to the porch and sat there decorously sipping, like old-fashioned ladies. The only discordant notes were the dusty toes of Portia's sneakers peeping from beneath her hem and the blunt careworn toes of Lucy's loafers peeping from beneath hers.

"Now about these summer cats," Portia reminded Mrs. Cheever.

"Yes. Mrs. Brace-Gideon's. *Her* summer cats. Every year she did that. She'd go to the Bullets' farm or the Hobbettsons' and pick up a couple of kittens. Dear little things. Then she'd take them back to the Villa Caprice and pet them and pamper them till September fifteenth, when she took them both to old Doctor Clisbee and had them chloroformed."

"No!" cried Lucy.

"How horrible!" cried Portia.

"That's exactly what we thought. Oh, I'll never forget Baby-Belle when she heard of it. She came straight to me. 'Min!' Baby-Belle said. 'Do you know what that horrible, awful, *fat* Mrs. Brace-Gideon does with her summer cats when she's through with them? She *kills* them, that's what!' Oh, Baby-Belle was wild! So was I. 'Why, she's a murderess!' I said. And Baby-Belle said, 'Well, I'll tell you one thing, Minnehaha Payton, she's not going to do it this year, because I'm going to steal them from her. So there!' 'Oh, Baby-Belle, you mustn't *steal* them!' I said, quite shocked, and she said, 'I mean *rescue* them, then.' 'But how?' I asked her, and Baby-Belle said, 'I don't know yet, but I'll think of something.' I knew she would, too.

"Now the thing about Mrs. Brace-Gideon was that she was so—oh, I don't know how to say it exactly—but when I think about her, remembering her, she reminds me of a big ocean liner—or, no!—of a *battleship*, yes, a battle-ship, just going forward and going forward while everything else gets out of the way: all the little boats and the fishes and the people in swimming. Everything. She wore a corset similar to the one you saw today, but more so. It just plain divided her in the middle so that she looked like a stout figure 8. Her face was very red—"

"Probably because she was so squeezed," Lucy said feelingly.

"Probably. She was what you might call *imposing*. Yes, indeed she was. Her hats were loaded with roses or plumes, and her fingers were loaded with jewels: oh, diamonds as big as *that!* Rubies! An emerald like a spoonful of mint jelly! And she had a lot of necklaces looped over her chest: Venetian glass beads, pearls, gold chains. There was a sort of *solidness* about her. I can't describe it. Even her hair, the way she wore it, looked solid, like one of the round dark loaves of pumpernickel we used to see at the Vogel-harts. . . .

"Well, this is how she was. She had a lot of help, of

course, though she lived alone; and whenever it came to
her attention that a plate or a cup had been chipped, she'd
call in the maid she thought responsible, point to the
chipped cup, and say: 'See this?' And then she'd dash the
plate or cup to the floor so it smashed and say: '*That's* all
it's worth to me once it's been chipped. Now sweep up the
pieces!' "

"My!" said Lucy.

"She sounds worse and worse every minute," said Portia
happily.

"Yes, she was a character. Not all bad though; of
course not. She was just so walled up in money she'd lost
touch with the way people are. One thing she loved to do
was to sing; she'd been trained to be a singer in her youth.
So once every summer she gave a musicale at the Villa Caprice. All the fathers dreaded it and grumbled about going,
but the mothers seemed to enjoy it, and the little girls both
dreaded *and* enjoyed it. (Boys were seldom invited, being
considered too risky as an audience.) The girls dreaded the
thought of sitting still all that time, fighting off giggles,
and they enjoyed the prospect of the ice cream and little
fancy cakes that would come afterwards.

"Every musicale was about the same. For instance, it always seemed to be a lovely day when all the fathers
wanted to be outdoors playing tennis or sailing. Everybody was uncomfortable in his best clothes, and there were
little uncomfortable gold chairs to sit on.

"Mrs. Ravenel always opened the concert by playing a
piano solo, and she did it in a very fancy way, shooting up
her wrists and flashing her rings and twitching her eyebrows. We had our first trouble with giggles then and
there. I remember my sister Persy kept biting her pigtail
to keep from bursting out, and I would have to pinch my
leg till it hurt. Oh, it was a terrible struggle!"

"I felt like that the time in church when a dog walked
up the aisle and then sat down and scratched his ear," said

Lucy. "Thump, thump, thump. Right in the middle of the sermon."

"Ah, then you know what it's like. But after Mrs. Ravenel had twitched and glared through a piece or two, Clay Delaney would play some songs on his mandolin, and we all loved him and nobody wanted to laugh then. After that there'd be something else, Mary Humboldt playing on the harp or Mr. Vogelhart seesawing away on his violin. That wasn't funny, only boring, and Baby-Belle said it caused her to itch all over like chicken pox. *Then* Mrs. Brace-Gideon would come sailing in like a battleship and start to sing." Mrs. Cheever began laughing helplessly. "Oh, it was so—oh, she was so . . ."

After a moment she continued. "Even her voice was solid! Enormous! Strong! Hard! She sang in German and she sang in French, and when she sang in English, it didn't sound at all like American (though she came from Pittsburgh); it didn't even sound like *English*. All her necklaces would tremble and glitter, and the glass things on the chandelier began to shake, and we shook, too, with our held-back giggles. Sometimes I would try to fix my mind on something sad. My Uncle Thomas was killed at Appomattox, I would think to myself. And though I'd never even known my Uncle Thomas, the thought was often sufficient to stop the laughing.

"Well. Now. *That* summer, the one I'm talking about, the musicale happened to come right after we'd heard about the fate of the summer cats. Oh, you should have seen Baby-Belle! When it was Mrs. Brace-Gideon's turn to sing, *she* didn't need to giggle. No, indeed she did not! She just sat there, Baby-Belle did, with her arms folded on her chest staring at Mrs. Brace-Gideon severely, like an Indian chief or a judge or somebody like that. And on this day Mrs. Brace-Gideon was wearing one of her big loaded hats. (Afterwards I heard my father telling my mother that it put him in mind of a New England boiled dinner.) So every time she held onto a high note, the brim of the hat would jiggle heavily. Even then Baby-Belle didn't want to laugh, and looking at her I didn't want to either.

"The funny thing was that afterwards Mrs. Brace-Gideon came up to Mrs. Tuckertown, *sailed* up to her, and said: 'Baby-Belle seems to take a real interest in music. Why, when I was singing, she was just as *absorbed—!'* "

"How about the cats, though?" interrupted Portia. She didn't mean to be rude, but she was worried.

"I'm coming to them. So *just* as the ice cream was brought into the dining room, and *just* as the beautiful little cakes were set out on silver trays, Baby-Belle came up to me and hissed into my ear: 'Come on, let's get the cats!' '*Now?*' I said. 'I'm hungry. They've got chocolate and vanilla and pistachio and fresh peach!' 'Look here, Min,' Baby-Belle said, 'this is life or death. Now's our chance.' So I said, 'Oh, dear. All right.' Baby-Belle could be very masterful.

"She was perfectly right, too. It was our best chance. Everybody was eating and talking: gabble, gabble, gabble. The cook and the coachman and whoever was left in the kitchen were having their own party: gabble, gabble, gabble. Baby-Belle and I ran through the flower garden, where all the hollyhocks had paper blossoms. (Mrs. Brace-Gideon would not stand for having her hollyhocks stop blooming; she made new crepe paper flowers for them and stuck them on with glue.) Then we ran through the vegetable garden.

" 'Where are we going?' I asked Baby-Belle. 'To the coach house where the cats are,' she said. But when we got to the coach house the doors were locked!

" 'Mean old thing,' said Baby-Belle. 'I suppose she thinks one of her guests might steal her precious old landau or her precious old runabout.'

" 'Maybe she's afraid they'll steal her cats,' I said, and

Baby-Belle just looked at me and said: 'Once and for all, Min, this is rescuing and *not* stealing! And there's an open window, so come *on!*'

"Now Baby-Belle and I were dressed in our best, of course. I had on a white dotted-swiss and that eternal sash; but Baby-Belle's dress had come from Paris, France, and it was white *lace:* dozens and dozens of little real lace flounces! Baby-Belle didn't give a hoot; she flung her leg over the window sill. 'Baby-Belle, you'll ruin your dress from Paris, France!' I said, and she just said, 'Pshaw, who cares? This is a matter of life or death!' And she scrambled and squeezed her way into the window, and I was such a coward that I didn't follow her. I just stood there quaking and pretended I was standing guard. And then Baby-Belle was suddenly sticking a kitten out of the window and saying, 'Here, take it!' 'Where's the other?' I said. 'Gone up on a beam, but I'll *get* it,' she said. And then there was a terrible noise of scrambling and panting and, I'm afraid, some swearing, and then an awful thud. I was afraid Baby-Belle was killed, but she wasn't. She stuck the next kitten out of the window and said: 'Take the confounded thing! They certainly make it hard to rescue them!' She looked very mad and red and hot. Her hair ribbon was untied as usual, and when she climbed out of the *window*, I nearly screamed! Oh, she was a spectacle to behold! Those lace flounces! All hanging down in tatters and festoons! And her stockings were torn and her legs were scratched, and she was covered with dust. But, 'Come on,' she said. 'We'll have to go out past the greenhouse.'

"It seemed to me that we'd been gone for an age, but it must only have been a short time, because when we pushed our way through the hedge and ran along behind it, we could still hear gabble, gabble, gabble, coming from the Villa Caprice.

" 'Where are we going *now?*' I said. I was out of breath from running, and the kitten kept clawing my neck.

'Craneycrow,' Baby-Belle said. 'We'll hide them there and take food to them every day.' Now I thought that was inspired! 'Baby-Belle, that's an inspiration!' I told her, and she said she thought it was, too.

"When we got to the Tuckertown boathouse, she told me to wait there with the kittens, and when she came back a little later, she had changed her dress and combed her hair and looked respectable again. As respectable as she ever *did* look. 'And I swiped a bottle of milk for the kittens, too,' she said.

" 'But what will they say when they see your dress from Paris, France?' I asked her, and she said: 'Oh, they won't see it for a while. I stuffed it up the chimney. And when they *do* find it—well, I'll think of something.' That was Baby-Belle all over: 'Sufficient unto the day is the evil thereof.' That was *her* motto."

"And did you get the kittens to Craneycrow all right?" asked Portia.

"Yes, indeed we did. They didn't care for the canoe ride at all. No, they did not. But when we had put them in the house and fixed them a bed and given them a bowl of milk, they settled right down, good as gold.

"We took the boys into our confidence that evening, and they agreed to supply us with fish. So every day after that, rain or shine, we rowed or paddled over to Craneycrow to feed the kittens. Milk, chub, shiners, black bass; oh, those creatures never lacked for a thing; they grew sleek and fat. And then when the time drew near for us to leave Tarrigo, we took Ben Gateway into our confidence, too. (He was the old man who raked the walks and pruned the hedges.) And he found good homes for both those cats, bless his heart.

"So every summer after that, as long as we were all at Tarrigo, Mrs. Brace-Gideon's summer cats would vanish mysteriously sometime between the end of August and the middle of September. It became a real puzzle to the grownups. 'I can't account for it at all,' Mrs. Brace-Gideon told Mrs. Ravenel. 'But it does save me the bother of a trip to Clisbee. I think it must be Providence.' "

"You and Baby-Belle were Providence, all right," said Portia. "But for the kittens, not for *her!*"

"Maybe we benefit from the providence of others more often than we know," suggested Mrs. Cheever.

Lucy scraped up the last of the sugar at the bottom of her glass. "I like the sound of Baby-Belle," she said. "I bet she would have been for the Giants."

13

GONE-AWAY DAYS

The bridge was nearly finished and, to the surprise of everyone, was turning out to be very pretty. They had expected it to be useful, sturdy, well-made, but not exactly pretty. However the Castle's fancy railings gave it an ornamental air, and its span was graceful above the Gulper.

"It looks like a Japanese picture we have at home," Julian said. "But *that* bridge is red."

"Good. We'll paint this one red, too; why not," said Mr. Payton. "Then nobody can miss it."

"Maybe we should christen it, too, Uncle Pin. We could have a celebration, sort of. And I think it would be only fair if everyone, every single one of us, waited and crossed over together right after that, and went to explore Craneycrow."

This was really very noble of Julian, and nobody knew it better than he did.

So when the bridge had been painted, and the paint had dried (a great deal of it on the clothes of the builders), a ceremony was held. Mrs. Cheever attended wearing a broadcloth suit trimmed with soutache braid and a hat with a warped peacock feather. Lucy wore a long red dress from the ball-gown trunk and a short velvet opera cape trimmed with iridescent beads. Portia was striking in purple taffeta and the necessary Roman sash. Mr. Payton and the boys were dressed informally, as usual, Foster and Davey still more informally and rather dirty besides; but over all the group there was a radiant air of festivity.

Julian had brought a bottle of ginger ale for the occasion.

"But are you sure ginger ale is the right thing?" asked Portia.

"Why not? We have to use something. Champagne's to christen boats with; water's to christen babies with. What do you think we *should* use? Chocolate milk?"

"Crazy," said Portia.

The air had that dimmer sideways light that one sees on late summer afternoons. A breeze that carried a cool touch of autumn rustled among the reeds, and the reeds sounded dryer. Julian presented the ginger ale bottle (which was wearing a necktie of red ribbon) to Mr. Payton.

"Will you—uh—officiate, sir?"

"Delighted. Honored," replied Mr. Payton, accepting the bottle. He turned to the waiting group. "Ladies and gentlemen," he began. "Also goats, dog, cat, duck, chickens, crickets, hornets, frogs, snakes, birds of the air, and anybody else within earshot—"

"You forgot mosquitoes," Foster said.

"Yes. Thank you. Also mosquitoes, caterpillars, turtles, sleeping bats, and the skunk that lives under the Humboldt house, and anybody *else* within earshot, it is now my solemn duty to christen this bridge—" He lowered the bottle. "Julian, what the deuce are we naming this bridge?"

Nobody had thought of that. There was a pause.

"Why don't you just call it the Gulper Bridge?" suggested Foster logically.

"Excellent. That all right with all of you? Very well. Bridge, in the name of the Philosopher's Club and the inhabitants of Gone-Away Lake, I now have the honor to christen you the Gulper Bridge!" With that Mr. Payton brandished the bottle and knocked it hard against the railing. Glass sparkled and flew; ginger ale trickled fizzling into the moss.

Foster spoiled the solemn effect, though, by suddenly shouting: "Last one over is an old dead horse!" and then leaping across the bridge with Davey at his heels.

Next, in a stately procession, came Mrs. Cheever, Portia, and Lucy, each holding her skirts up daintily and rustling. Next came Mr. Payton and the three big boys. The bridge stood up nicely under the strain, swaying gracefully, and at the point above the quaking bog, quaking in an alarming but interesting way.

Foster, who naturally had a proprietary feeling about the island, stood at its edge, holding back the needled branches for Mrs. Cheever as if he were holding back a portiere.

"How the place is overgrown! I can't believe that we used to be able to see Craneycrow Cottage right across Tarrigo!"

"We'll see it again, soon," Mr. Payton assured her. "For our next project is to cut down a few of these trees at the front."

Foster, reaching the little house first, opened the door.

"This is it. This is where I was," he said. "Come on in."

"My heavens, it does look witchful!" Portia exclaimed. And she thought to herself: If *I'd* had to stay here all alone in a bad thunderstorm, I would have died, that's all. Just died.

"Boys, help me get some of the shutters open," said Mr. Payton. "Witches hate daylight; it's a well-known fact. Makes their hair curl. They can't stand that."

With the shutters folded back, the room took on a more cheerful appearance.

"I'm going to bring a broom next time I come," said Portia. "This place makes me want to housekeep."

Lucy was sniffing vigorously. "I like the way it smells. It smells of pine needles and oldness."

"But come and see the kitchen that I found," Foster demanded. "The kitchen's neat!"

"Well, not neat exactly—" objected Mrs. Cheever, stepping in.

"I mean it's keen," said Foster.

"Oh," said Mrs. Cheever. Then she said: "Good gracious, how this takes me back! Look, girls, see that saucer still on the floor in the corner? It must have been used by the last of the summer cats—"

"Hey, Uncle Pin, look!" cried Julian. "Look what's carved on the table top! It's Tarquin again!"

"Well, by Jupiter!"

"What's a Tarquin?" asked Davey.

"It's the name of a dog we've got," Foster said. He sounded puzzled.

"Yes, but first it was the name of a boy I knew long ago," Mr. Payton told him. "One year he saved up enough to buy a knife of Swedish steel. And then he started glorifying his name; carved it here, you see, carved it on fences, carved it on the Philosopher's Stone—(though not with the knife)—and no doubt there are still trees in the woods that carry the news of his name!"

"This is a keen little house, Foss," said Davey. "I wish it was ours."

"You children must think of it as yours, mustn't they, Pin?" said Mrs. Cheever. "An extension of the Philosopher's Club."

"Maybe Foster and Dave *could* sort of own it, couldn't they?" Julian asked the others. "I mean it would be everybody's, really," he added hastily. "But it could be theirs more in a way, because of Foster finding it and all."

"Oh, *boy!*" Foster gave a short jump into the air.

"Oh, *boy!*" echoed Davey. "We can bring our stuff here, Foss. I'll bring my chemical set and my Martin Marauder."

"I'll bring my ray gun and some things to eat," said Foster.

"But one thing you must remember," Mr. Payton admonished them. "You are to come here *only* by way of the footbridge; you are to leave here *only* by way of the footbridge. There is to be no more trifling with the Gulper! Ever!"

"No, *sir!*" promised Foster from his heart.

"No, *sir!*" promised Davey, not quite from his heart but meaning it all the same.

The quiet reaches of Gone-Away were quiet no longer. At first there was the intermittent chopping of axes, and then the silvery groaning of the crosscut saw, and then the voices calling "*timber!*" The green trees fell majestically, one by one, until Craneycrow Cottage stood revealed, and sunlight could enter it once more.

"We'll let the trees lie where they are; they make an added safeguard against the Gulper," said Mr. Payton. "Heaven knows, we don't need them for firewood; we haven't even begun to use up the Castle Castle yet, and after that we've got the Humboldt carriage house. Excellent firewood. Plentiful."

Gone-Away was all alive again: not only where the boys were working, but where Lucy and Portia sat gabbling together in the sleigh or up in the branches of the Vogelharts' willow; and on the island of Craneycrow, where Foster and Davey popped in and out of their house, as fiddler crabs pop in and out of sand holes. When Mrs.

Cheever sat mending on her porch, she kept a careful eye on them, and so did Mr. Payton as he tended to his stock and garden. But the little boys were not aware of this. They played their noisy games, enjoyed their battles, pursued their projects, happy as kings and twice as independent.

So the month moved slowly in all its gold toward September. The wild cucumber vine that cloaked the Castle rubble was studded now with green seed-pods thorned and plump as porcupine fish.

"Later on when they dry up, they look like little purses of woven straw," Mrs. Cheever told the girls. "When I was a child, I used to pick them and stitch one end together with yarn, and make little braided yarn straps to hold them by, and then all my dolls had pocketbooks. I used to leave the seeds inside for money."

In the bog garden the yellow-crested orchis with its yellow feather and the white-fringed orchis with its snowy one had blossomed exquisitely and faded, but the grass-of-Parnassus still nodded star-shaped flowers.

Mrs. Cheever showed Portia and Lucy the place between swamp and woodland where there were scarlet cardinal flowers, each a bold chord of color, and near them their cousins, the blue lobelias.

"Oh, but if you could be here at the time of the fringed gentians! This lobelia is a lovely blue; yes, indeed it is. But the blue of the fringed gentian is the color of heaven!"

The swamp itself now carried large floating patches of purple, magenta, and yellow. The purple and magenta were ironweed and loosestrife and joe-pye weed, and the yellow was the beginning of goldenrod.

"And that means the beginning of fall," sighed Mrs. Cheever. "And so much still to be done, so much still to be picked!"

A great deal had been done already, and the girls had

helped to do it. They were the ones who had climbed the chokecherry trees and shaken the fruit down into an old sheet; and they had helped to harvest the beady elderberry plaques to be made into jelly and wine. Mrs. Cheever had made preserves of blackberries, blueberries, rose hips, and everything else she could lay her hands on. There seemed no end to the things that needed to be harvested, and some of them were strange indeed. The roots of boneset, for instance. "Good for a fever," said Mrs. Cheever, "although we seldom *have* fevers." And the leaves of joe-pye weed, to be dried. "Good for rheumatism," she said, "although we seldom *have* rheumatism. However, it is best to be prepared."

"Yes, indeed it is," agreed Portia, sounding so much like Mrs. Cheever that Lucy laughed.

The stalks of angelica had been cut and candied long ago, and a tray of hyssop flowers was drying in the attic.

"Later I'll make hyssop tea of those," said Mrs. Cheever. "I'll boil them with water and sugar. A wineglassful is excellent for a touchy stomach."

"Everything that grows seems to be eatable or usable," said Lucy.

"And some are deadly poison," Mrs. Cheever told them with relish, sounding like a witch herself. "There by the swamp, that thing that looks like a poor relation of Queen Anne's lace: *that* one is water hemlock, and the root of it can kill a man in the prime of life!"

"But it doesn't look at all poisonous," objected Portia. "It just looks boring."

"Many killers have a quiet appearance," said Mrs. Cheever, sounding more like a witch than ever. "Jimson weed is an exception, though. You'll see some of those in Judge Chater's old pheasant-run; they're horned and thorned the way a poison plant *ought* to be." She straightened up (she had been cutting mint). "Yes, the world is a remarkable place. Think of it, right here, right in plain *view*, there are weeds that can kill and weeds that can cure and weeds to live on and weeds to make cats happy!"

"Let's go look at that Jimson weed," said Portia.

But they didn't go just then because they heard Foster come drumming across the Gulper Bridge. (That bridge made a very nice noise when you ran on it.) Foster came running and drumming. He was holding something up and yelping for Uncle Pin.

"Look what *I* found, Uncle Pin!" He was yelping. "Where are you, anyway?"

Davey came running and drumming just behind. "Lookit what *he* found, Uncle Pin!"

The little boys had spent a happy day at Craneycrow. All their days there had been happy so far. In the first place it was pleasant to occupy a house in which nobody ever told you to pick anything up. Just because of this, now and then they *did* pick things up; now and then they even used a broom.

Another nice thing was to eat your lunch sitting on the Gulper Bridge in the sunshine without anyone to tell you to eat your crusts. Now and then because they were so hungry, they *did* eat their crusts, but usually they just dropped them onto the Gulper, where they would linger awhile before sinking.

And their island had many things to offer besides the cottage: the woods that smelled so sweet; the pale little crowds of Indian pipes and the orange jack-o'-lantern mushrooms that pushed up the needles. There was a broken rowboat at the northwest end of the island, which could be used as a Lockheed F-90, a rocket ship, an atom-powered submarine, and sometimes even a rowboat.

Also there was such an abundance of turtles that Foster and Davey had started what Julian called a Turtlearium.

They had built a rather informal pen of chicken wire, and in this enclosure a melancholy assortment of turtles crawled about looking stonily at each other, scrabbled in and out of a pan of water, and were fed meat and lettuce from the boys' sandwiches. Sooner or later they managed to escape. Foster and Davey always caught more, though, or perhaps they caught the same ones over again. It was hard to tell.

"There isn't much differentness about these turtles," Foster said. "Except if they're red-and-black or if they're yellow-and-black."

"And in the bigness of them," said Davey. "Some are fathers and mothers and some are children, I guess. Just the way everybody is."

But on this day they did find a turtle that was different.

They had been looking for arrowheads on the west bank of the island, where there was a tiny cliff with stones and pine roots sticking out of it. Everytime they found a more-or-less triangular stone, the one who saw it first would say: "Man, this really is one!" or: "Yikes! This *has* to be one! Look at the sort of whittle marks!" In his heart of hearts each boy knew that none of the stones was a real arrowhead, but it was fun for a while to believe that he believed.

"Wait a minute; there goes another turtle," cried Foster, scrambling up the bank and seizing the poor creature, which was out for a walk. "Come on, Turtly, I got you!" The turtle prudently took its head, legs, and tail indoors with it. Foster dusted it off on his jeans, turned it over, and yelled.

"What?" said Davey.

"It's got writing on it, lookit! T-A-R-Q-U-I-N! Tarquin! Like on the kitchen table. The boy Uncle Pin was telling about, he even carved his name on *turtles!* And there's numbers, too."

"Let me see!" Davey, who could read better than Foster, wrested the turtle from his friend and looked at the numbers.

"Eighteen-ninety-one!" exclaimed Davey. "Man, this is an old turtle!"

Foster wrested the turtle back again.

"Come on; we have to show Uncle Pin!"

As they galloped across the island and across the bridge shouting, they attracted all the attention they wished.

There came Portia and Lucy and Aunt Minnehaha, with their hands full of flowers and leaves. There came Uncle Pin with his bee-veil flapping. Julian and Joe could be heard thundering down the Bellemere stairs, and Tom Parks, very dusty, emerged from under the front steps of the Delaney house, where he had been trying to fascinate the bull snake. (Tom called himself a "herpetologist," which really means he was a snake specialist.)

Uncle Pindar read the turtle.

"Well, by Jupiter!" he said in awe. "Well, by Jove! *I* remember this fellow. I remember Tark carving on the shell. Look, Minnie—"

"Yes, but please don't call me Minnie," said his sister.

"Look here, this turtle was mature when Tark caught it. Why, it must be as old as I am! Maybe older. I wish," said Uncle Pindar with a rueful sigh, "I wish I were as well preserved as he is!"

"I think you're better preserved!" said Foster warmly. "And you're better looking, too."

14

THE VILLA CAPRICE

And then finally, there was nothing anyone could do about it; it was September. Soon it would be time for school. The one that Portia and Foster went to never opened till the middle of the month, but Julian's would start right after Labor Day and Lucy's a week later. Soon she would be going back to Albany, where she lived.

The nights were cold and still; great lights roved over the North, and the stars shivered. In the mornings there was a nap of hoar frost on the grass, but by the time they reached Gone-Away it had melted, except in the shady spots. All the reeds were glittering, and the foxtail grasses were full of rainbow sparks. Already the swamp maples had turned scarlet.

"Did you ever notice how people call leaves leaves all the rest of the year but in the fall they call them foliage?" said Julian.

Everything pointed to the fall. The trees and thickets whistled with starlings, and swallows arranged themselves on telegraph wires like the notes in a stave of difficult music. Foster said there was a bird in the woods that sounded sad.

"It says 'T.V., T.V.,' and that's all it says."

"We used to think it said 'Phoe-be, Phoe-be,' " said Mrs. Cheever, "but who can tell a bird what he's saying?"

"If it's a boy bird, it's probably saying 'See me, see

me,' " said Portia, and Julian put out his large foot and tripped her up.

When they walked through the swamp nowadays, they had to wear their boots (slop, slop) and look out for cobwebs.

"This is the season of the spider," Mr. Payton said, and it was certainly true. Everywhere, tossing among the reeds, were little beaded cloths of web, and now and then they came on a larger kind, each wearing a dressy black-and-yellow spider and marked with a silky track as if the artist had signed his name.

"These nights when I go out to see if the stars are all in the right places, I take my flashlight with me," said Mr. Payton, "because this is the time when the big night spiders come out. Their webs are high up, fastened to tree branches, to the clothesline, to the shed roof, and anchored to the earth with guy wires tall as you are. And right in the middle of each one sits a big pale spider the size of a fifty-cent piece."

"More the size of a quarter," said his sister. "But that's big *enough!*"

One afternoon a few days before Lucy was to leave, she and Portia took a walk in the woods behind Gone-Away. They had never explored them and thought they'd better do so before it was too late. Besides, the swamp had seemed strangely still. The big boys were back in school, and the little boys had been taken by Mrs. Blake to have their hair cut. Mrs. Cheever was busy making wild-grape jelly, and Mr. Payton had decided to take a nap.

"T.V.," sang the sad bird in the woods.

Portia and Lucy walked beneath the silent trees. There was no wind, and the sky was clouded. It wasn't going to rain because Mr. Payton had said it wasn't, but it felt as though it might be going to at any minute: the air had that cool, waiting feeling.

"Skarp, skarp," called a crow high up and far away. On

the quiet air a leaf, and then another, sidled downwards.

"It's too *early* for them to fall," said Lucy indignantly.

"No, it's not, darn it," said Portia. "Oh, I *wish* it was just the beginning!"

"So do I," said Lucy with a loud sigh. "Is this a path, Porsh—I mean Portia—or do I imagine it?"

"Maybe an old road. Let's see where it goes."

Sometimes they almost lost the trail it was so over-grown, but they managed to keep to it, and after a while Lucy said: "I think we're coming to something. Yes, look, there's a wall!"

"And there are gateposts!" said Portia.

These posts were taller than the girls were and richly wrapped in poison ivy. Peeping from between the scarlet leaves, they could see square raised concrete letters, like the letters one sometimes sees on tombstones. Portia picked up a twig and carefully lifted the ivy aside to read them.

"Villa Caprice! Lucy! That's Mrs. Brace-Gideon's house! The one that's never been opened in all these years; let's go see it!"

"Okay, but maybe it's spooky. Those trees ahead look spooky."

"Oh, I think they just look interesting. Come on."

Beyond the posts there was what must have been a driveway once, but it, like the road leading into it, was al-most entirely overgrown. As Mrs. Cheever had said, the woods had captured the Villa Caprice long ago; and the thing that made many of the trees seem spooky was the fact that they were draped and festooned with matted honeysuckle vines, so that they looked less like trees than like great shawled figures, stooping, or like sinking vessels wrapped in their sails.

"My, it certainly is quiet, isn't it?" remarked Lucy in a loud hearty voice.

"Sh-h, yes it is. But you only make it quieter if you yell like that," said Portia contradictorily.

"Why did she have to have all this road, I wonder? My goodness, where's the *house?*"

"I think we're coming to it, I see something—"

The trees thinned out a little, and rounding a curve, they came to a stop. There in a clearing, up to its sills in weeds and briars, stood the Villa Caprice.

It looked like a huge lumpy rock at the bottom of the sea, for all of it, all its turrets and bay windows and battlements and balconies, was smothered under a vast green vine. And beyond the house the privet hedge, grown tall as trees, curved over in a dark wave.

"Gee, I think it looks spooky, don't you?" said Lucy.

"A little bit," Portia admitted. "But now that we're here, Lucy, I do think we should go and look at it. Maybe we can find a way to peek in."

"I guess we should," agreed Lucy doubtfully.

As they waded through Michaelmas daisies and wild asters, the crickets popped and scurried.

"Aunt Minnehaha says owls live in the porch," remarked Portia.

"Oh," said Lucy, who was not at all certain how she felt about owls, or how owls felt about people.

The porch steps were under an arched porte-cochere that squatted on four cobblestone pillars.

"Are we going up on the porch?" whispered Lucy.

"Certainly," whispered Portia, who was really rather scared and dubious about the owls herself.

The porch ran around two sides of the house. It was broad, with a broad railing. More cobblestone pillars supported the roof, and the Boston ivy hung down from the eaves in a green curtain. The porch floor had a deep resonance under their feet, even though they tiptoed. In the litter of old leaves and bitten acorns there were droppings and owl feathers, but they saw no owls.

"I guess they've gone south," said Portia, and Lucy heaved a sigh of relief.

There was no possible way to peek into the house. Mrs. Brace-Gideon had taken no chances. The windows were boarded solidly. The front door was not only boarded but barred with iron bars.

Still tiptoeing, Lucy and Portia left the porch by the side steps and made their way through the brambles to the back of the house. But there again the door was barred and boarded.

"Heck," said Lucy, who was no longer feeling worried. "What in the world did she *keep* in this house? Diamonds or something?"

"I just wish I knew."

But when they came around to the west side of the house, where there was no porch, Lucy gave a shriek: "Look!"

Portia saw that one of the three boardings on a bay window had fallen away from its rusted nails and lay loosely against the vines that supported it. Without further comment the two girls charged through the tangle to the window and wrenched the boarding free of the vines; it fell heavily, hitting Lucy's toe, so that she had to hop and groan for a minute. And when she stopped groaning about that, there was something else to groan about, because there were shutters under the boarding and they were wired together.

"But I think," said Portia, "if we got a stone or something—the wires look pretty rusty."

"But do you think we should?"

"Oh, why not, it doesn't belong to *anybody*. And we can wire the shutters together again. Oh, Lucy, I'm just *dying* to see what it's like inside!"

"Me, too," said Lucy, tossing scruple to the wind.

They found a useful stone and an old piece of metal near the locked-up carriage house, and then they went to work to pry the wires apart, which turned out to be very easy since they were so rusted. The girls seized a shutter in their hands and tugged until it creaked forward grudgingly. Then they bumped heads in their eagerness to look in.

They saw nothing. Before she left, Mrs. Brace-Gideon had given orders for every shade to be drawn.

"Darnation!" said Lucy.

"She thought of *everything*," said Portia. "My heavens, what a suspicious woman!"

Exhausted and cross, they sat down among the weeds. Portia picked a grass stem and bit it while Lucy took inventory of the scratches on her arms. It was very still in that place. Both of them suddenly noticed how still it was. The crow was gone; even a little plane that had been humming across the sky was gone. When a falling leaf ticked against the grass, they both jumped.

In the gray light Lucy's face looked greenish and solemn. "I think—" she was starting to say, still whispering, when suddenly, shockingly, from inside the locked-up house, from the house that nobody had entered for more than half a century, came a hideous noise! Just once they heard it: the sound of a piano, but not the sound of music. It was the harsh discordant noise someone makes if he brings his fist down on the keys in anger.

"Help!" gasped Lucy.

"Hurry!" begged Portia; but they were already hurrying. They were leaping through the weeds with their hearts bucking in their chests. Lucy caught her foot in a honeysuckle vine and sprawled her full length; but no sooner had she landed than she was up again, running. Not until they reached the gateposts did they slow down, and then not very much.

"That house is haunted," Lucy gasped, jogging along by Portia. "That was a ghost!"

"Oh, there aren't any ghosts," said Portia. "I don't think there are. Maybe it was a robber."

"How'd he get in though? It *must* be a ghost!"

"We've got to tell Uncle Pin right away!"

"Oh, I know. But I just have to stop a second and catch my breath!"

"Well, catch it quick," panted Portia, looking nervously over her shoulder.

And then as luck would have it, they emerged from the woods at Gone-Away just in time to see Mr. Payton driving off in the Machine. They shouted frantically, but of course he couldn't hear them above his own stupendous racket.

"What's up?" inquired Julian's voice from Mr. Payton's kitchen.

"Oh, thank goodness *you're* back!" cried Portia, bursting in.

Julian was seated at the kitchen table. He was gazing raptly into a jar that contained a caterpillar five inches long, and his face had the tender look of a mother watching her sleeping babe.

"Look, Porsh; it's a Citheronia regalis and it's—"

"Wait, Jule, listen! Someone's gotten into the Villa Caprice!"

"Or some*thing*," said Lucy ominously. "I think it's ghosts!"

"What are you two *talking* about?" demanded Julian, never removing his eyes from the spiky monster in the jar.

When they had explained fully, and only then, did Julian tear his gaze away. A look of joy was dawning on his face.

"Come on! Let's go!"

"Wh-where?"

"To the Villa Caprice, natch."

"Oh, Jule, wait for Uncle Pin, or get the police or something."

"And waste *time?* Nonsense!" said Julian, sounding elderly. "Tom's here; we'll take him."

"Lucy and I'll just wait here with Aunt Minnehaha," said Portia.

"Listen, we need you to show us the way, brain."

"Oh, dear," said Lucy. Then she got her first real look at the caterpillar and screamed.

"The only dumb thing about you, Lucy, is the way you react to caterpillars," said Julian. "Well, come on, let's go get Parks."

"Shouldn't we tell Aunt Minnehaha?"

"I don't think we ought to worry her," said Julian considerately. He really feared that Mrs. Cheever might object to the expedition if she were informed of it. "Now let's see. I've got my Scout knife, and I guess I'll borrow Uncle Pin's flashlight—is there some way to get into the place?"

"There's that window," quavered Portia.

"Okay, and I'll borrow the hatchet for Tom. I wish I had a gun."

"Oh, dear," said Lucy again.

Tom Parks, when they called him, emerged from under the Delaney's front steps wearing the bull snake around his neck.

Lucy screamed again apologetically. "It's just all these awful *things*," she explained. "The awful noise and the awful caterpillar and the awful snake! I hope I'm not going to have a heart attack."

"You might have one. In about fifty years," said Julian callously. "Come on, Parks, file away your friend, there's work to do."

"Heck, *more* work?"

But when he heard what it was, Tom's face also took on a look of joy.

By the time they had reached the gateposts Portia and Lucy absolutely declined to go any farther.

"You just follow the track; you'll come to it," said Portia. "And the window's on the unporched side."

"We'll be able to hear you if you yell," added Lucy helpfully.

"And come galloping to the rescue, I bet."

"We can go *get* help, though."

"Chicken, both of you. Well, so long, nice knowing you," said Julian cheerfully. He and Tom trudged manfully away.

"Oh, dear," said Lucy.

"Gee. It *doesn't* look very inviting does it?" said Tom a few minutes later, staring at the big leafed-over house. "Not what I'd call cozy, brother."

"You going to be chicken, too?" said Julian, who was feeling far from heroic himself. The place was so still! But Tom assured him that he was not.

"It's just that I can see how the *girls* must have felt," he said, fingering the hatchet at his belt.

They tiptoed cautiously through the weeds to the west side of the house, where they found the unboarded window easily. There they waited for a few minutes holding their breaths and listening, but there was not a sound.

"Anybody home?" called Julian at last.

No answer, of course. No sound at all.

"Well, here we come, ready or not!" he shouted, with a boldness he didn't quite feel.

"Window's locked," said Tom.

"We'll have to break a pane then and reach in to unlock it the way they do on TV," said Julian; and he picked up the stone that Lucy had dropped, threw it against a pane, which broke accommodatingly, put his hand in, and turned the catch.

"Now," he said.

Together they worked the window open, but it was a struggle. Then Tom reached in to raise the shade, which leaped from his hand and flew up to its roller with a terrible bang.

"The girls will think we've been shot," prophesied Julian, and sure enough there came Portia's panicky voice: "Jule, what *happened?*"

"Just the window shade," he bellowed reassuringly. "Come on, Tom, let's go in. You want to go first?"

"After you, my dear Alphonse," said Tom, bowing.

The breath of the house was dank and cold. First Julian, then Tom, hoisted himself over the sill, reached a leg down cautiously, and stepped on the tufted cushions of a sofa. Dust rose in a cloud.

"How could even dust get in?" Tom wondered.

"It just does. It gets everywhere."

In the ivy-filtered light from the window they could see that they were in a small room, perhaps a study. There was a desk, a glass-fronted cabinet containing trapped sets of books, and on one wall were many water-color sketches of Venice and cathedrals and things like that.

The door of the small room stood open, but when they went through it, Julian turned on the flashlight, because the large hall in which they found themselves was very dark.

To the right of them stood the big front door, its transom blocked by the boarding outside; and to their left a broad staircase curved upward. It had a stout oak balustrade, and on the newel post stood a bronze lady four feet tall who was wearing what looked like a wet sheet and some bunches of grapes. Her face was wreathed in a dimpled bronze grin, and she was standing on the toes of one foot. The other foot was lifted archly in the air, and above her head she was holding a torch with a fringed lampshade on it.

"She looks like Miss McCurdy, the cashier at the Blue Premium," said Tom, laughing. "But I sure never saw Miss McCurdy *acting* like that!"

He and Julian were in fine spirits, interested in all they saw, and no longer worried at all.

"Girls are always *imagining* things," said Tom.

"Oh, I guess they can't help it," said Julian kindly.

The rest of the hall loomed with dark pieces of furniture. Beside the front door stood a blistered green umbrella-stand with some very elderly umbrellas still in it, and next to it was a coat rack covered with claws and dragons' heads and pineapples, or things that looked like pineapples. Julian was so interested in this that he didn't see the cast-iron pug dog at his feet and fell over it. He came up covered with dust; a velvet of soft dust lay thick on every surface.

An arched doorway yawned on darkness at the opposite side of the hall, and he and Tom stepped in daringly. The searching beam of the flashlight showed them a large room full of shadowy objects; there was a gleam of gilt from the heavy frames of dark oil-paintings, and from the bandy legs of little chairs. On the floor stood a big shrouded thing shaped like a lopsided heart. "A harp, maybe?" said Julian. And from the ceiling hung another shrouded thing, like a giant wasps' nest. As they walked forward on the gritty floor, the wasps' nest tinkled.

"That's a whatchamacallit; it's a chandelier," said Tom brightly.

There was a fireplace with a ruffle hanging from the mantel, and the mantel itself was heavily populated with china figurines, candelabra hung with prisms, a clock that had said half-past three for half a century, glass bull dogs with rhinestone eyes, a bronze cobra with turquoise eyes, and a photograph of Theodore Roosevelt in a tarnished frame.

"I bet he was a good chewer," said Tom.

"Look at that red-and-gold piano, man!" exclaimed Julian, switching the light away. And just as he said the words, he remembered that it was the sound of this piano that had terrified the girls; and just at the very instant he was remembering this, the flashlight went out in his hand.

It was black as pitch.

"Hey, what happened?" Tom sounded anxious.

"Battery, I guess. Maybe I did something to it when I fell."

"Maybe it was—" Tom's voice was low. "But I don't believe in ghosts, do you?"

"Na-a. Ghosts shmosts," said Julian, hoping he sounded tough.

They felt their way toward the door, the big black room tinkling faintly as they moved, and then—what was that? There was a wild scrabbling across the floor, a scurry of claws, and something scampered right over Julian's feet. Julian yelled and rushed into the harp, which fell with a clangorous jangle to the floor. Worse still, he lost his head, turned in the wrong direction, came to what he thought was a wall, but the wall gave way at his touch and turned into many cool strands of small objects that clattered like rain on a tin roof.

"TOM!" roared Julian.

"Here, this way, here's the door," called Tom shakily. "You okay?"

"I don't know. A thing ran across my feet, I don't know what. Let's get *out* of here!"

"I'll never say I don't believe in ghosts again," promised Tom. "I *do* believe in them now, *honest* I do," he assured the house, hoping to placate any spirits that might be at large.

But once in the study, and the blessed daylight, the fear was gone; for they were just in time to see the soft willowy leap of a squirrel, first to the sofa and then to the sill of the open window, where it paused for a moment sitting on its haunches. It looked at them once, looked out at the daylight, and then with an emphatic quirk of its tail, as if this were a comment of some sort, it leaped to its freedom.

"The ghost!" said Julian, ready to laugh or cry and doing neither. He felt about half his actual age, which would have made him younger than Foster.

"Gosh. Well, for a minute, gee, I really almost thought —" said Tom sheepishly. "How do you suppose it got in, though?"

"Down the chimney. Fell down, maybe, and couldn't get up again."

"Jule?" came Portia's voice from outside. "Oh, Jule, where *are* you?"

He leaped to the window. "We're all right, Porsh! And the ghost was only a squirrel. Listen, the house is *great*. There's a red piano, and chandeliers, and everything!"

"But wasn't it *scary?*"

"Na-a. Who's afraid of a little old squirrel! Listen, let's come back tomorrow and bring everybody!"

"And plenty of flashlights, too, brother," muttered Tom.

After they had stopped at Gone-Away and told Aunt Minnehaha and Uncle Pin about their adventures, and after they had left Lucy and Tom at the red sock, Portia and Julian walked wearily home.

"I feel as if I'd been to war," said Julian.

"Me, too," said Portia.

"And you know something else, Porsh? I wouldn't tell anybody else, and if you ever *dare*—"

"Oh, I won't, I won't!"

"Well, I really was scared. I was chicken as anything. I yelled. I bet you heard me."

"Well, *I* think you were just terribly brave," Portia said. "If *I'd* been in that place with the dark and the squirrel and everything, I would have died, that's all. Just absolutely died."

15

THE VILLA CAPRICE AGAIN

On the next day, which was conveniently a Saturday, a garrulous procession wound its way along the blurred trail that led to the Villa Caprice. First came Portia and Julian; then Lucy, Tom, and Joe; then Mrs. Cheever and her brother, who was swinging his cane jubilantly; and then the other grownups: the Blake children's father and mother and their Aunt Hilda and Uncle Jake. Last of all came Foster and Davey zigging and zagging even more erratically than usual because Foster had the puppy, Gulliver, on a leash. Gulliver was the dog that he and Portia had chosen for their own.

"I can't believe I'm really going to see the place again!" Mrs. Cheever exclaimed. "Just think of it, Pin! More than half a century, more than half a hundred years! I declare!"

In the sunny morning light and in the company of grownups the trees no longer seemed spooky at all; and the Villa Caprice, when they came in sight of it, just looked old and lonesome; rather pathetic.

"How I love privet that's grown up like that," said Portia's mother, and her father reaching into an apple tree said: "Russets! The best eating apple in the world; why, I haven't tasted one of these since I was a kid."

The human beings were not the only creatures to break the silence of the place; a crowd of starlings had invaded the privet and swung there chuckling and hissing, and blue

jays squawked in the oak trees. Besides that, everywhere, over and under every other sound, was the sound of the crickets, but one no longer heard it any more than one's own breathing.

"It's funny how you never notice when they start," Julian had said. "All of a sudden they're just there."

"Look, chrysanthemums!" cried Portia's mother, breaking off a crimson sprig. "They need cutting back, but what a lovely color they are."

"I see an old busted glasshouse back there, Foss," said Davey. "Come on, let's see!"

Off they went in the speckled sunshine with Gulliver pulling Foster this way and that way like a big strong fish on a line.

"I've never seen such a vine," said Portia's mother. "How old do you suppose it is?"

"Oh, old!" Mrs. Cheever told her. "Mrs. Brace-Gideon planted it when I was a small child. It was very irritating to her because it would not grow fast enough to suit her. Natural growth was very irritating to her anyway. It took its *time* so."

Portia wondered how in the world Mrs. Cheever was going to climb through the window; she was wearing a black silk dress with a slight train, and a shawl with a long fringe, which had collected a number of burs.

"Hilda, isn't that a monkey-puzzle tree?" said Portia's mother, pointing. "I swear it is! Honestly! A monkey puzzle!"

That was a tall queer tree that rose clear of its honeysuckle shrouds, brandishing many limbs as bristling as bottle brushes.

"Everything about this day seems like a dream," Aunt Hilda said. "The hazy light, that weird tree, the whole *place*—"

"A nice dream or a bad one?" asked Portia anxiously. She felt about the Villa Caprice the way Foster felt about

Craneycrow—responsible for it, in a way; she wanted people to like it.

"Oh, a pleasant dream," her aunt assured her. "The kind where everything is peaceful and a little bit better than real."

Well, it seems real as anything to me, thought Portia.

"Nothing dreamlike about *this*," complained Uncle Jake a moment later as he stepped up on the porch and fell through it. "Ouch," he added, climbing out and bending over to pick the splinters from his socks. Luckily he had not fallen far; the porch was less than two feet off the ground.

Everyone walked gingerly after that, but still the floorboards boomed and quivered underfoot.

"Not sound," said Mr. Payton, knocking on the floor with his cane. "And no wonder after all this time. Roof'll be sound though, I wager. Made of slate."

When they had walked around the rear of the house to the bay window, Mrs. Cheever felt misgivings.

"Oh, I don't know, Pin. Do you think we ought?"

"We're neither vandals nor thieves, Minnie! We'll just have a look around, then close it up again."

"Well . . . oh, all right. I'm just as anxious as you are to see it."

Portia's father and Uncle Jake gallantly lifted Mrs. Cheever to the sill, where she drew her skirts and fringes about her and entered agilely. They heard her sneeze.

"Gracious, the dust!"

One by one they clambered over the sill, waiting till all were gathered in the study.

"Foster? Davey?" called Aunt Hilda, but the little boys were out of earshot.

Portia's father peered into the glass-doored bookcase, reading the titles of books aloud.

"*At the Mercy of Tiberius. Vashti. Three Roads to a Commission in the United States Army. Angela, A Tale of*

Sacrifice. A Guide to Carriage and Wagon Painting. And *Mme. Vavasour's Gypsy-Witch Fortune Teller!*"

"Evidently Mrs. Brace-Gideon was a woman of varied interests," observed Uncle Jake.

When they were all assembled, they went on into the hall, well lighted now by a volley of flashlights.

"Great Scott!" said Portia's father, transfixed by the bronze lady on the newel post.

"That's Miss McCurdy," Tom explained. "Hi, Miss McCurdy."

"Too many vitamins," was Uncle Jake's comment.

"Look out for the iron dog; he's bad to stub against," warned Julian. "Now this big room ahead is the one where my light went out and there was the squirrel and all."

"She called it a drawing room," said Mr. Payton. "Everybody else at Tarrigo had sitting rooms or living rooms or parlors, but Mrs. Brace-Gideon had a drawing room."

The battery of flashlights searched the big dark place. There was a feathery tickle of disturbed dust.

"I can't believe it!" cried Portia's mother.

"*Not* a Turkish cozy corner!" exclaimed Aunt Hilda. "*Not* a bead curtain!"

"That must have been the thing I walked through," said Julian, with a remembering shudder. "It felt like lots of little bones and knuckles. Ugh!"

He went over to examine the curtain. It was composed of many hanging cords on which were threaded small bamboo tubes and round glass beads. A few of the cords, worn through with age, had fallen to the floor and lay in little heaps. Julian played his fingers along the hanging strands, and there was at once a delicate sound of hail, or of rain on brittle leaves.

"It makes a keen noise," he said, rippling it again.

Joe said it reminded him of shaking the dice for parcheesi.

Portia and Lucy were fingering the ornaments on the mantel, and the grownups were exclaiming over everything in sight.

"I can't believe it!" repeated Portia's mother, staring at the piano that was red and gold and curly. Two carved fish-tailed ladies held up the corners of the keyboard.

Portia's father placed his hands on the keys and played a chord. A wild and twangling sound came forth.

"That's exactly the way the squirrel sounded," said Portia, "and he wasn't even trying."

"Ooh, were we ever scared!" Lucy said, and like Julian, gave a remembering shudder.

Portia's father struck another chord.

"I don't know whether this piano could be rescued or not. It's been neglected for more than fifty years by everything but moths and mice. It was a beauty once, though. . . ."

Uncle Jake had been strolling from one large oil painting to the next, recklessly dusting each one off with his handkerchief. He had viewed an elderly gentleman in a periwig, a scene of pyramids and sheep, and now he was confronted by the portrait of a lady.

"Now who is this? She must be a woman because she's wearing a dress and holding a fan, but she has the face of a Marine colonel."

Mrs. Cheever laughed her schoolgirl laugh, giggling into her hand. "Oh, that's Mrs. Brace-Gideon. Yes, indeed it is. A striking likeness!"

"She *does* look squeezed," said Lucy thoughtfully.

"And here's her particular chair," added Mrs. Cheever. "She used to sit there, straight as a ramrod, one little beaded slipper crossed over the other little beaded slipper. Oh, how well I remember!"

The chair was made of carved oak, with a high back and two stout oak ladies to hold up the arms.

"In that day women may have been called the feeble

sex," said Uncle Jake, "but they seem to have been chosen to shoulder the load. Women holding up gas lamps! Pianos! Even Mrs. Brace-Gideon!"

"Even mantelpieces," said Mrs. Cheever, lifting a corner of the ruffle above the fireplace; and there, sure enough, stood a lady carved of marble.

"Boys, let's see if we can get the front door open," suggested Mr. Payton. "If the nails have rusted in one place, they must have rusted elsewhere. And this house needs airing!"

The boys and the two other men followed him from the room, while the rest of the party went on exploring. There was a great deal to be explored: among other things a dining room with big broody furniture, and a kitchen with a big broody range.

"See how the cooking utensils are all in place," whispered Portia's mother. It was hard not to whisper in the silent, dust-veiled house.

"More and more like a dream," Aunt Hilda whispered back. Portia and Lucy began to feel creepy.

But just then came a very realistic noise of hammering and banging from the direction of the porch.

"It's my belief that that front door will defy them," predicted Mrs. Cheever, leading the way upstairs. They followed her in single file, touching the coated stair-rail gingerly. On the landing Lucy gave one of her screams, for there before them, in a vigilant attitude, stood a complete suit of armor, helmet and all.

"It's empty, Lucy," said Portia reassuringly, and when she rapped on the metal, it gave the clang of a cold radiator.

"This house is full of surprises," sighed Lucy.

"I know. The whole *summer's* been full of surprises. Nice ones, mostly; and that's the way I like it."

"I really do, too. Albany's going to seem awfully usual after all this."

Of the many rooms they saw upstairs, with their brass bedsteads, china washbasins, and framed steel-engravings, there was one that Portia and Lucy liked above all others. It was situated in the tower, a perfectly round little room, with a curved window and a curved window-seat beneath it. The wallpaper was patterned with faded forget-me-nots, and there was a small fancy desk with a key to lock it. If the blinds were open, they knew the window would look out across the grassy field and apple trees toward the gateposts and the woods beyond.

"Mother? Daddy? Where *is* everybody?" demanded Foster's voice from down below.

"Oh, the poor lambs, we forgot all about them!" said his mother.

"Coming, Foss," called Portia. "Wait till I show you!"

When Foster saw Miss McCurdy, he said: "What's she? An indoor Statue of Liberty?"

And when he saw the suit of armor, he said: "Man, what a robot!"

Later, when they all came down again, there was another surprise in store for them. As Mrs. Cheever had predicted, the front door had defied the men and boys, but they had managed to uncover one of the drawing-room windows.

Sunlight came in, and they were able to see the heavy webs that sagged from the wasps'-nest chandelier, the shredded crimson curtains at the window, and the dimming dust that lay on everything. But also they were able to see the pleasant proportions; that the room was lovely, or that it could be lovely.

"You know, if you took the awful porch off—" said Aunt Hilda.

"I know, I was just thinking," replied Portia's mother cryptically.

"And pruned the vines away from the windows—"

"And painted the walls white—"

"And had some nice cheerful curtains—"

"But if no one owns it—"

"Someone does own it, though," said Mr. Payton unexpectedly. "The state does, even if the state is unaware of it. The Doctrine of Escheat."

"The what of *what?*" demanded Mrs. Cheever.

"Doctrine of Escheat. If a house is left to no one, and no one claims it, after fifty years it automatically becomes the property of the state."

"Oh. We're really trespassing then, aren't we?"

"A little bit," admitted her brother. "But we've done no harm, and when we leave, we'll board it up again."

Portia's father was looking gravely at the photograph of Theodore Roosevelt. Still looking at it, he said: "I wonder what the state would ask for the place?"

And it was at that moment that Portia began to feel a hope she had never even thought of.

"Daddy, do you mean we might *buy* it?"

"Would you like that?"

Portia thought of the round room in the tower; of other rooms still unexplored; of the woods outside; and of *Mme. Vavasour's Gypsy-Witch Fortune Teller*. She pressed her hands together and looked earnestly at her father.

"Oh, Daddy!" she prayed.

"What about you, Foster?"

Foster thought of the greenhouse as an orbital space-station; he thought of the suit of armor, and the monkey-puzzle tree, and the sliding possibilities of the bannisters. He gave one of his short jumps.

"Boy! And Gulliver would like it, too."

"Where is Gulliver, by the way?"

"Tied to a tree; he's okay."

"The place is far enough from Gone-Away to be fairly well out of mosquito-range," said Mr. Payton.

"But not so far that you couldn't leave your hermitude to come and see us, is it, Aunt Minnehaha?" begged Portia.

"I should say it's just within my boundary line, thank fortune," she said, laughing.

"Thank fortune," echoed Portia.

One by one they climbed out of the window again, very dirty, all of them, even the grownups. They had agreed to come back after lunch and do some more exploring before they boarded up the house again. The sun was high; the haze had burned away.

"It doesn't seem like a dream now, does it, Aunt Hilda?"

"No," said Aunt Hilda, looking back. "Now I can see how it would look with the grass cut and the porch gone and all the windows showing. A nice, comfortable, *real* house."

"It'll be great if you do get it, Porsh," said Julian. "I bet these are swell collecting grounds."

"Maybe we could have a horse," said Foster.

His father put one arm around his shoulders, one around Portia's.

"You know, kids, there are at least seventy-two big 'ifs' between us and that house."

"Oh, more. A *hundred* and seventy-two," corrected their mother. "So, darlings, you really mustn't get your hopes up."

Yet she looked hopeful herself: happy and excited; and a few minutes later they heard her saying to Aunt Hilda: "I think yellow curtains would be nice."

"But *if* the state authorities agree," their father continued. "And *if* the price isn't too high, and *if* there's not too much repair work to be done, and *if* what there is doesn't cost a fortune, and *if*—"

But somehow—who knows how?—Portia and Foster were perfectly certain that every "if" would be overcome and that some day the Villa Caprice would be the Blakes' own house to live in every summer.

This prospect made Foster so happy that he had to run. He had to jump.

"Come on, Gull, old boy! Come on, Dave!"

Off they went, bucking and yelling, as wild as Tuscarora Indians.

Portia was affected differently. She felt very quiet with happiness.

"Oh, I just hope and pray," she said.

And Mrs. Cheever walking lightly beside her, said: "Well, I have a feeling, Portia, I have a feeling in my bones that your wish is going to come true."

"Do you, Aunt Minnehaha? Honestly? Cross your heart?"

"I cross my heart," said Mrs. Cheever. "Yes, indeed I do."